Temptation Isla

By

Lynda L. Lock

Dedication – Paradise Lost

Lawrie Lock; March 3rd 1942 – September 3rd 2018

Paradise is normally considered to be a place, but for me paradise is a person; my husband, adventure partner, world-traveler, lover and best friend - Lawrie Lock.

He was always my rock, my inspiration, my sounding board. We've traveled the world together getting into mischief, sticky situations and occasionally heated arguments that revolved around a finicky classic car doing something weird.

His recent diagnosis of Rapid Onset ALS caught us by surprise, and the speed with which Lawrie declined into complete paralysis took our breath away. But through it all he smiled that killer-gorgeous smile, and tried to make the best of a horrific situation. He slipped away on September 3rd 2018, at home, looking at the beautiful Caribbean Sea.

If the rain is liquid sunshine, then my tears are liquid love. I will love you to my last breath.

Chapter 1

September 16th Día de la Independencia

In the shadow of the city hall, el Palacio Municipal, a fit, muscular thirty-something man leaned in a deceptively casual stance against the large support column. Unencumbered, his powerful hands hung loosely at his sides. He had learned the hard way, never trap your hands by trying to look with-it. In a fight the cool dude with his fingers tucked into his pockets was the first one to get hurt. The watcher's dark hair was uniformly buzzed close to his skull, a number-two cut in barber-jargon. His symmetrical features would have been handsome if he smiled but, in his life, there hadn't been much to smile about.

The watcher, Alfonso Fuentes, scrutinized the crowd checking for anyone who was excessively interested in him. He was a trusted bodyguard for a Cancun drug lord, Rafael Fernandez, or as he was referred to *Don* Rafael, the respectful Spanish honorific title.

Temptation Isla

The celebration activities appeared to be normal for a national fiesta but because the life of a drug lord's henchman was frequently very violent and very short, he was watchful and wary like an often-kicked street dog. He had recently celebrated his thirty-third birthday which in this business was something of a rarity.

A little more than two weeks after the arrival of Hurricane Pablo on August 28th, the square in Centro on Isla Mujeres was still shabby. Many buildings needed paint. The palm trees were shredded, but still standing and would rapidly sprout new fronds. Some of the windows in surrounding complexes were covered by boards or hurricane shutters, but the square had been swept clean and decorated for the annual Día de la Independencia celebration.

There were tangled and worn strings of coloured lights criss-crossing the square. Loud salsa music pulsed through the crowd. At midnight the fireworks had boomed overhead showering celebrants with hot, hard plastic shards, the discarded casings from the spent explosives. Vendors offered cold beer, tequila, and hot food. Small Mexican flags were poked into upswept hair-dos, stuffed into pockets, or clutched in hands. Many islanders were dressed in an eclectic mix of anything green, white, and red — the colours of the national flag. The islanders had two reasons to celebrate; the Día de la Independencia, Independence Day, and their survival of Huracán Pablo. Life would go on.

Blending in with the locals celebrating Día de la Independencia, Fuentes wore black slacks and a red, linen Guayabera shirt. Under the long-sleeved shirt he wore what was commonly known as a wife-beater, a white sleeveless singlet. Trendy black leather shoes specially fitted by a shoemaker-cousin with thick metal toe-caps were polished to a high gloss. The shoes were handy weapons as was the folding knife resting in his right pocket. Around his neck hung two thick gold chains; one was weighted down by a heavy crucifix the other dangled a palm-sized dagger-shaped object. They were weapons disguised as jewelry.

Satisfied his perimeter was secure, he returned his watchful gaze to the small group of adults and children whose concentration was focused on the scene in front of them.

A ruggedly handsome man was positioned in the traditional romantic stance, down on one knee with an open black-velvet box extended in his left hand. The man had just proposed to a tall slender woman whose café-au-lait skin flushed with happiness.

"Si! Si! Yes, I will marry you, mi amor." She shouted happily as tears over-flowed her dark green eyes and streamed down her cheeks. A mass of curly hair grazed her shoulders, the light bounced off the natural blonde highlights that ran through her dark tresses.

The man sprang up, with a whoop of happiness, and slid an engagement ring onto her finger.

Fuentes heard the man say, "I promise to love you until my last breath," as he crushed her in a passionate kiss. Their friends cheered and clapped and whistled.

Fuentes, the watcher, knew the woman's name was Yasmin Medina, and she was twenty-nine years old. Many of the old-time island gossips were convinced that this woman strongly resembled another woman born in the 1860s. Martiniana Gomez Pantoja, nick-named La Trigueña or the brunette, also had sea green eyes and dark, blonde streaked hair. La Trigueña was the object of unrequited love for the Spanish sea-captain-turned-pirate Fermin Antonio Mundaca de Marecheaga. However, unlike Martiniana Gomez, Yasmin Medina was obviously deeply in love with her paramour Carlos Mendoza.

Fuentes also knew quite a bit about Mendoza and his pals. The man was edging towards forty and Fuentes supposed the women would consider him handsome. He was lean and muscular, with deep brown eyes, short black hair, and the sun-darkened complexion of his Maya ancestors. A faint scar ran from his left eyebrow to the corner of his mouth, acquired during a knife fight when he was in his early twenties and was edging towards illegal activities. Rumour had it that shortly after the incident Mendoza had straightened out his life and had become an upstanding island citizen as well as a successful business man. He owned the popular and very successful *Loco Lobo Restaurante* on Hidalgo Avenue. Fuentes was certain Mendoza's success had made him complacent and careless, he wouldn't be a problem.

As much as he respected and feared *Don* Rafael, Fuentes privately questioned the reason for this assignment. This small group of insignificant islanders that he was currently observing, had recently enraged the *Don* by temporarily disrupting his drug-dealing business on Isla Mujeres. He didn't thing the situation was worth the risk, but apparently his boss thought otherwise. He wanted payback. He wanted to teach the islanders that meddling in his business had deadly consequences.

Fuentes thought the group had unintentionally stumbled onto the connection between the death of a local taxi driver, Ricardo Villarreal and *Don* Rafael's foot-soldiers Edgar Valdez and Fernando Sánchez. The two men didn't do a thorough job of disposing of the body and now the policía were investigating. To remove any connection to himself and the murder *Don* Rafael had ordered the deaths of Valdez and Sánchez.

Fuentes ran his thumb and forefinger over his luxurious moustache. Only his boss was allowed to goad him about the appearance of his precisely groomed facial hair. *Don* Rafael had smirked as he pointed at Alfonso's moustache telling him it looked like batwings glued to his face. Any other person who dared to ridicule his appearance learned that enduring pain quickly followed their short-lived mirth.

His gaze flicked again to the group he was watching. His flat stare settled on the pretty woman in the centre of the group, and he felt his manhood stiffen in response. She was a strikingly beautiful woman. She shouldn't have aggravated *Don* Rafael.

Chapter 2

September 17th

Jessica Sanderson rested her hip against her kitchen counter thumbing a message to her parents in Canada. "Yasmin and Carlos are getting married! I'm her maid of honour. You're invited. Can you come?" She flipped her long blonde plait over her right shoulder and twiddled with the end. It was a childhood habit that inexplicably annoyed her mom.

A few seconds later her phone announced an incoming Facetime call. "Hi honey," her mother said with a smile.

"Hi Mom," responded Jessica as she guiltily dropped her hand away from her braid.

"A wedding, how exciting," responded Anne Sanderson, "Please give Yasmin and Carlos our congratulations."

"I will, we're all thrilled for them. Will you and Dad come to Isla?" Jessica studied her mom's face in the tiny screen thinking, *that's probably what I will look like in another twenty-five years.*

She and her mother shared similar features, bright blue eyes, thick blonde hair and slim builds. Anne Sanderson's trim body had filled out a little as she had pushed past her fiftieth birthday now nearing fifty-six years old.

The one characteristic they didn't share was an interest in tattoos. Jessica had arrived home one Christmas with a vibrant full-sleeve tattoo on her left arm depicting the sea life of the Caribbean including turtles, dolphins and a whale shark. Her mom had just shook her head, and said wait until you are older and that fancy artwork fades and hangs in wrinkly folds from your chicken-wings; her mom's pet name for flabby under arms.

Her mom still worked full-time as an emergency room nurse in the Vancouver General Hospital and remained strong and fit, if just a little rounder in the hips and thighs. In the corner of her eyes the inevitable signs of aging were appearing. She felt deeply and her face displayed her emotions for the world to see, ranging from exasperation with bureaucracy, to sorrow for her dying patients, and the intense love for her family.

"Are you sure we're invited? We've never met them." Her mom sounded perplexed.

"They really want to meet my wacky family. Heaven only knows why." Jessica joked, pulling a comical face.

"When are they getting married?"

"Friday February 22nd, two days before Yasmin's birthday and the week before Carnaval starts."

"Won't the island be jammed with tourists?"

"Absolutely, but Yasmin and Carlos want everyone to have fun while they are here, so Carnaval is a perfect time." Jessica agreed, before adding, "There will be dozens of dance troupes, and parades, and a charming pageant with seven or eight different sets of kings and queens."

Anne huffed a laugh, "Why so many? Can't they make up their minds?"

"Every age group from the pre-schoolers to senior citizens has a king and a queen. Sometimes the principal royalty of the Carnaval are minor celebrities such as Cancun TV personalities." Jessica waved her right hand excitedly as she tried to convey her enthusiasm to her mom. "Mom, you'll love it! Please come."

"Let me talk it over with your dad. We'll have to see if we can get time off work."

"You and Dad have seniority, of course you'll get the time off." Jessica countered. "By the way, Matt and Jake are included in the invite," she said referring to her two older brothers who along with their father were professional firefighters in

Vancouver Canada. "Yasmin and Carlos really want to meet everyone."

"Are you sure you want those two pranksters meeting your friends?" Her mother asked with laughter in her voice.

"Yes, they really liven up a party!" Jessica quipped. "Seriously Mom, everyone is included. Matt and Jeff will fit right in, especially with Diego my Isla brother." She said referring to her good friend Diego Avalos.

"You certainly have talked a lot about him in the past," Anne Sanderson laughed good-naturedly. "So, does that mean I have another son to feed?"

"No worries there. Diego is married to Cristina, and they have four beautiful kids. Cristina is an outstanding cook who always makes enough for an army." Jessica smiled as she remembered how in the after-math of the hurricane her island friends and their families had gathered for a riotous and lively dinner at Diego and Cristina's. "I've mooched meals at their house a few times."

"Jessica, you are as hopeless as your brothers." Her mom replied, "You've always hated cooking."

"Nope, don't hate cooking. Just can't be bothered," Jessica retorted with a smile. "Jake and

I are the lazy ones. Matt is an amazing cook. The crew at the fire hall love his creations."

"Yes, and sometimes I think he gets his promotions based on the gourmet meals he whips up." Anne sighed, "He never showed much interest in cooking when he was a grocery-devouring teenager."

"Hormones Mom, strictly hormones. Eat, sleep and obsess about girls. That's all a teenage boy does."

"You weren't so different yourself. Eat, sleep and obsess about boys."

"Yeah, yeah. Whatever."

"If we do come we'll finally get to meet Sparky, your famous pooch." Anne said.

"Yes! And you'll love him." She responded referring to her terrier-mix, low-rider mutt that was well-known on the island for his bravery and his extraordinarily sensitive nose.

Jessica couldn't decide whether it was her fault that she and Sparky had recently been involved in several sketchy escapades, or whether he was the one leading her astray. He was becoming something of an island personality, a short-legged hero. When the two of them buzzed around the island in her recently purchased second-hand golf cart, more people recognized him then her. She couldn't count the number of times people would yell, *Buenos Días Sparky!* And then sheepishly add *Hola Jessica*.

"From the photos you have posted on your Instagram and Facebook pages I can see he is a handsome dude. Those mischievous deep-brown eyes, floppy ears, and curly coat. He's a sweetie."

"Yes, he is. He's my boy." Jessica agree as she reached down to caress his long Spaniel-type ears. Sparky seemed to know that she was talking about him and rolled onto his back, demanding a tummy rub. She complied, crouching down and running her hand back and forth over the thinner fur on his chest and stomach.

"By the way, what about Auntie Pattie? Do you think she would like to join in the festivities?" Jessica asked.

"I don't know Jess. That seems like you are stretching your, *I'm the maid-of-honour,* authority a bit too far by including my baby sister in the celebration."

"Pattie is my favourite of all my aunties. We've always been more like sisters than aunt and niece."

"Don't I know it," her mom laughed. "The two of you were always scheming behind my back."

"I'll check with Yasmin first, then if it's okay, I'll call her and ask her to come to Isla."

"Okay honey, let me know. I'm looking forward to the wedding, although I am concerned that the Crazy Canadians will be a little overwhelming for the other guests."

A joyful laugh erupted from Jessica. "Mom, you have no idea how fun and extravagant a Mexican *boda* can be. You are in for a real treat." She said her voice rippling with laughter. "Love you, bye."

Chapter 3

September 17th

Fuentes stood in front of *Don* Rafael's expansive desk, made from rare jungle woods originating in the Yucatan. As always when he stood waiting for instructions from his boss the beautiful wood captured his interest. Dramatic streaks of dark-chocolate brown contrasted with the golden-yellow tones in the dense, heavy pieces of lumber cut from the Zapote trees. He'd like to own such a beautiful piece of furniture, some day.

His hands were lightly clasped behind his back, his legs were braced shoulders-width apart. Parade rest, his old Sergeant had called it. After his eighteenth birthday he had completed two years of mandatory military service in the Mexican army. It was boring and hard physical work, but it trained him to be patient and observant. It also taught him to research and plan his assignments thoroughly.

"How many?" Fernandez asked.

"In the group there are fourteen adults, an equal mix of both men and women, plus six young children." When giving his report he had learned to keep his eyes focused on the Fernandez's chin, slightly subservient and non-threatening.

"And there is a wedding, *una boda*, planned?"

"Yes sir, Carlos Mendoza, the owner of the *Loco Lobo Restaurante*, is marrying one of his employees, Yasmin Medina."

"When?"

"February 22nd."

Fernandez leaned forward resting his elbows on the polished wood, tapping his finger-tips together as he considered the information. "Take them all out! At the reception." He said, sweeping his right hand in a side-ways motion as if he was knocking a pile of papers from his desk to the floor.

"As you wish, *Don* Rafael." Fuentes' jaw muscle twitched with tension.

"You don't agree." Fernandez said.

Fuentes paused momentarily considering his next words. He had to get this exactly right or he would, at the very least, be demoted to the riskiest tasks or in the worse-case scenario killed for insubordination.

"Permission to speak freely, *Don* Rafael?"

"Cut the fake military crap, Alfonso, just say what you are thinking."

Depending on Fernandez's mood the flick of a finger or a chin pointed at a victim could quickly end that person's life. At the moment there were just the two of them in the office but only a shout away were several younger enforcers, who were keen to remove the *old dude* thought to be blocking their upward advancement in the ranks. He knew. He had once been one of those hungry wolf-pups eager to remove the aging alpha male.

"Yes, sir." Fuentes said, "As you know, since its creation in 1976 the federal and state politicians have spent millions promoting Cancun as a mecca to temptation. Like Las Vegas the abundance of cheap alcohol, casual sex, and illicit drugs tempts the visitors to misbehave in ways they would never consider in their hometowns. If we cull one or two of the trouble-makers the news reporters will have their attention-grabbing headlines for a day or two and then move on to the next tragedy."

He paused gathering his thoughts, then continued speaking. "If we eliminate a group of islanders, plus their children, we will cause a storm of international media attention. The tourists will be terrified and stop coming to Cancun and maybe even to Mexico. Your companies need the tourists."

Fernandez smiled coldly at his employee.

"With respect sir, I am not telling you how to operate your businesses. I am only suggesting that a less dramatic gesture might be easier for the tourists to accept."

"What do *you* suggest?" Fernandez asked, sarcastically.

"I will remove the central personality of the group and make it clear to the others why that person was killed. The rest will rapidly fall into line when shown the consequences of meddling in your affairs." Fuentes kept his gaze steady, not quite making direct eye contact but not avoiding Fernandez's glower.

"Alfonso," Fernandez said, the tone his voice demanding his subordinate's complete attention. Fuentes lifted his gaze slightly to meet the man's cold glare, "Do it. If you screw up. You will be replaced."

Carefully keeping his expression neutral he responded, "*Claro*. I understand." *Replaced* was *Don* Rafael's euphemism for a slow and painful death.

~

"*Jefe*, got a minute?" A short round-faced man called to Carlos as he strode towards his office at the rear of the *Loco Lobo Restaurant*.

Carlos veered towards the kitchen, "Qué pasó, Juan?" He asked his head chef.

"We've lost another refrigerator. That one." Juan pointed with his chin keeping his hands and eyes on the food he was preparing.

"What happened?"

"We had another power outage last night. When the power came back on the fridge didn't."

"*Mierda*," He cursed, "that's two this month."

"More gifts from our friend Pablo."

Carlos nodded. He knew Juan was referring to the recent flooding during hurricane Pablo. Salty water plus high humidity equaled corrosion and electrical problems for the appliances. Carlos cursed as he tugged on the appliance trying to pull it away from the wall. "The damn wheels are frozen with rust."

"Daniel," He motioned to the dishwasher a young skinny kid barely fourteen-years-old, "Give me a hand with this."

Daniel grabbed one side, Carlos the other and they were able to walk the refrigerator forward enough that Carlos could squeeze in behind. He fiddled with the reset button on the surge-protector, also known as a circuit-interrupter, the device that was supposed to protect equipment against sudden power spikes. *Not much of a help in this case.* He unplugged and reconnected the device. Still nothing.

"Useless piece of junk," He muttered, nudging the metal device with his foot. "I'll call Santiago, maybe he can fix the fridge."

"*Jefe*?" Daniel asked in a quiet voice.

"Si?" Carlos poked his contact list, searching for Santiago's number.

"My dad is an electrician. May I try something before you call the repairman?"

Carlos stopped fiddling with his cellphone, and looked at the teenager. "Okay, go ahead." Carlos stepped aside and let him slip behind. Daniel unplugged the protector, and inserted the refrigerator plug directly into the outlet. They heard the unit kick on. Carlos laughed and opened the door to confirm it was functioning properly.

"The circuit-interrupter did its job, *jefe*, it protected the refrigerator. But you need a new interrupter."

"Great job, gracias." He bumped fists with Daniel, planning to give him a little bonus in his pay envelope as a thank you. He was relieved that a new surge-protector would only cost about three hundred pesos instead of twenty thousand pesos for a new fridge.

Casting a guilty glance at his office, Carlos veered towards the bar. He would treat himself to a Diet Coke and a smooch with Yasmin, avoiding the stack of paperwork on his desk a little longer.

"Hola mi amor," He said, sliding behind the bar. He scooped ice into a tall glass and filled it to the brim with the sweet, dark liquid.

"I would have done that for you." She gave him a long, lingering kiss.

"Mmmm, I'll take the kiss instead." He said, then pointed at the walls. "The new photos look fabulous."

"Si, I think we chose well."

He perched one butt-cheek on a bar stool as he sipped his Coke and studied the interior of the restaurant. Only three weeks after Hurricane Pablo things were almost back to normal. The large colourful photos by Tony Garcia were dirty but they had survived. A few years ago he had found a place in Cancun where for not much money he could get the photographs printed on *lono*, a tough out-door vinyl instead of paper. He could have cleaned the vinyl and frames and then rehung them, but it had been a good opportunity to update the images.

A week ago he had poured two glasses of wine, one for Yasmin and one for himself and they had opened Tony's Facebook page. After an hour of clicking through the thousands of beautiful photographs they had chosen six new images. He and Tony had settled on a price, and by the end of the week the walls were vibrant once again with scenes of everyday island life.

The interior of the restaurant had easily withstood the powerful category five storm. Built of concrete walls, wooden ceiling beams, stamped-concrete floors, and granite counter-tops the *Loco Lobo* was almost indestructible. The cobalt blue and lime green vinyl-covered chairs were scrubbed clean, and looked presentable despite the amount of mud and seaweed deposited by the storm surge. The fourth wall was an intricate metal security gate operated by an electrical motor. It was rolled up during business hours, allowing more seating in the street. Damaged by something large and heavy during the storm the security grille had been the first item to be replaced.

After few days of intense cleaning, the restoration of electrical power to the island, and the resumption of the ferry services the *Loco Lobo* was back in business.

Yasmin had hinted it was time for a complete do-over later in the year. There was no time and no money for restaurant renovations until after *la boda*. He still hadn't replaced his car, his beautiful black Porsche 911 that had been crushed by a concrete power pole.

Even though it was insured the Porsche might never be replaced, more likely his next vehicle would be something practical and family-friendly; otherwise known as an *old-fart's car*. Diego frequently reminded him Yasmin wasn't yet thirty and she just might want a family.

Carlos rested an elbow on the granite counter top and propped his chin in his hand, contemplating the lovely woman he was going to marry in six months. His first marriage had been a disaster and he had been single for so many years he hadn't given much thought to having a family, until now.

"Hola, beautiful. Could I take you out for a drink after work?" He asked, winking suggestively at her.

"I'm sorry sir, I don't date customers." Yasmin dead-panned.

Chapter 4

September 28th Cancun

"What time does the shipment arrive?" Rafael Fernandez snapped at Fuentes.

Alert to the tone in Fernandez's voice Alfonso instinctively straightened in his chair. He supressed the urge to jump to his feet and salute. "It is scheduled to be here at ten this evening, *Don* Rafael."

Rafael Fernandez checked his computer screen again, "Good, no moon."

"Si, *Don* Rafael. That is why I chose this date." Fuentes agreed. He consciously willed his breathing to slow down. He needed to stay calm and be clear-headed when dealing with his unpredictable boss. "But, the forecast has changed to high winds and rain." He held up his iPhone with the Intellicast weather page displayed.

"Alejandro Sánchez is a good seaman. He'll be fine." Fernandez countered. "He has a good strong boat, and four large Yamaha outboard motors."

"Si, claro," Fuentes agreed, "If the shipment gets delayed we still have two more nights of darkness, tomorrow night and the next night."

"How many this time?" Rafael demanded.

Fuentes briefly studied his boss. He had lost interest in discussing the weather or the amount of moonlight. His primary concern was money.

"Twenty. Two males and eighteen females."

"Are the females useable?" He asked, meaning useable as sex-slaves in the hundreds of illegal brothels located in the larger cities of North America. Even large sporting events like the annual Super Bowl was a good source of business for the industry. The American gangs brought thousands of under-age girls and young women into the host city during the annual testosterone-fuelled event. At one Super Bowl event a police sting operation labelled, *The National Day of Johns*, had arrested six hundred people and taken sixty-eight women into protective custody. Fernandez didn't care he had already been paid and he had a lucrative deal with the Russian mafia bosses to supply replacement females.

"I've been told they are all young and healthy, but I haven't seen any photographs."

26

"It doesn't matter what they look like. Age is the only thing that matters to my buyers," Fernandez replied without a flicker of emotion. "Why the two men?" He demanded. "Why not four more girls?"

"Primarily to keep the girls under control, but they also paid ten thousand American dollars each to get out of Cuba."

"Wanted by the policía Cubano?" Fernandez asked his subordinate.

"Si," Fuentes nodded.

"Bien!" Fernandez said, a feral grin on his face. "Then their ride just got a little more expensive. They can work off the extra by doing a few jobs for me."

Fuentes thought the idea of using two unknown Cuban criminals to work within their tightly-controlled organization was not a smart decision, but he kept his mouth shut, his face blank. He had already expressed his disagreement over the idea of a massacre at the upcoming marriage of Carlos Mendoza to Yasmin Medina. Contradicting *Don* Rafael again, would be incredibly stupid. The man was paranoid and psychotic.

~

A thirty-five foot cabin cruiser drifted slowly off of the eastern side of Isla Mujeres. The motors were quietly burbling as a group of residents indulged in the experience of a night dive, frolicking with turtles and other sea creatures.

José Avalos, Diego's cousin, had asked Jessica to be the spotter, to help him find the divers when they resurfaced. She was doing it as a favour to José, refusing to take any money for helping out. She knew that his family needed every peso that he might make from the charter.

She'd tried diving once, and discovered she hated it. Her right ear wouldn't equalize and the pain had caused her to rapidly gulp her air supply. She only lasted about ten minutes before signalling to the dive master that she was returning to the surface.

Her only regret was not being able to complete her dive. The plan was to visit the underwater museum, *Museo Subacuático de Arte*, built near the Manchones reef between Isla Mujeres and Cancun. There were approximately six hundred statues sunk in the ocean at three separate locations. The statues depicted life, both the negative and positive aspects, in the Maya world from the beginning of history until present day. They were made from a special type of concrete that encouraged the growth of coral, seaweed and algae which would eventually attract marine life. It was an attempt to pull tourists away from the over-taxed natural reefs along the Maya Riviera.

"Get down! Now!" José whispered harshly.

"Why?" Jessica asked.

"Shhh, get down now." He pushed his hand down, indicating to lay flat on the deck, as he ducked below the level of the console.

In the blink of an eye, an unlit high-powered boat sped past leaving only a wake to indicate it had been real, not imagined.

"Traffickers." He said, slowly standing up.

"Why did I have to hide?" Jessica asked, pulling herself to her feet and staring at the dark, empty ocean.

"They are not nice people," José looked at her with an odd expression, adding, "and you're a beautiful woman."

Jessica opened her mouth to ask more questions when a diver popped to the surface. Her focus switched back to the task at hand, "Diver at six o'clock." She said, and pointed behind them.

~

The sleek vessel, with four large Yamaha motors, lightly bumped against the dock in a Cancun marina. The deck-hand stepped onto the concrete finger-wharf and wrapped the bow line to a cleat, and then looped the stern line. He gave a thumbs up sign to the captain, Alejandro Sánchez. *All secure.*

Sánchez shut down the motors and hissed "Quiet!" at the young females to halt their nervous chatter. "Silencio."

He turned around and saw eighteen pairs of dark, uneasy eyes watching him. It was the same every damn time.

The girls thought they were headed to the promised land of the United States to work as nannies, or domestic workers for wealthy benefactors. Alejandro knew they were anxious about their futures, but were happy to work and send money back home to help their large and extremely poor families. *Don* Rafael's advance man in Cuba watched as elementary-aged females became teenagers, and then approached their parents offering a chance at a better life if they would consent to letting their daughter move to the USA.

As a dad, he loathed this job, but as a family man trying to provide a nice house, good education, and the ever-more-expensive things that teenagers demanded, Alejandro did whatever it took to earn a living. No one, not even his beloved wife, knew that he worked for *Don* Rafael.

She thought he was helping poor Cuban refugees escape a tyrannical government and start a new life somewhere in North America. His children thought he was a hard-working fisherman, labouring all night to pay for their private school educations. They were so pre-occupied with their latest expensive electronic gadget, or updating their social media sites, that they never questioned why he didn't stink when he returned home from *fishing*.

He had warned his wife time and again, never, ever tell anyone that he was bringing people from Cuba to Mexico. Either way, supposedly helping refugees, or bringing in under-age sex-workers, he was a criminal. If caught he could be jailed for the remainder of his life. Mexican jails were tough, dangerous places unless the prisoner had money to ensure his comfort and safety. Stacks of money, like *Don* Rafael.

"What now?" A deep guttural voice asked.

Alejandro's eyes briefly cut towards the taller Cuban who said his name was Victor. "We wait. The transport will be here soon. Just keep still and be quiet."

"We don't need transport," the man said, lifting his duffle bag and preparing to step over the gunwale. "We have friends."

Pulling a pistol out from under the console Alejandro pointed it at the taller Cuban. "Stop!" He demanded. "*Don* Rafael wants to chat with you and your buddy."

The man slid a glance at his friend. He had his hands held away from his body in an open non-threatening gesture. He pointed with his chin at the deckhand.

Alejandro knew without looking his helper had another pistol trained on the second man who called himself Ciro.

"Why the guns if *Don* Rafael just wants to chat?" Victor demanded.

"We are just making sure you don't leave without paying your respects to our boss." Sánchez answered, noticing a set of familiar headlights sweep into the parking lot. "The truck's here. Don't do anything stupid, or I *will* shoot you."

Chapter 5

October 10th Afternoon Isla Mujeres

"Are we having a stag for Carlos?" Diego Avalos asked. He throttled back on the twin twelve-hundred horse diesels engines of the *Bruja del Mar*, slowing her into an easy cruising speed. There was no rush to get back to the marina. Today was a shakedown cruise for the *Bruja,* her first full-day out in six weeks. Everything was operating perfectly.

The fifty-eight foot Viking sport-fishing boat was co-owned with his brother-in-law and working partner Pedro Velazquez. Their fishing and photography charters had died off after Hurricane Pablo as tourists avoided their damaged community.

Bruised and beaten, but not down for the count the island was now back to about sixty-five percent efficiency and thanks to his eleven-year-old tech-savvy son, their business was improving. José had created Facebook, Twitter, Pinterest, and webpage ads. He even sent out regular email updates to previous clients encouraging them to book their next trip. The first group was scheduled for next week. José detested school lessons, but he was a little genius with social media.

Pedro displayed a big toothy grin, "Remember his stag when he married Elena?"

"That was hilarious!" Diego said. His deep laugh boomed across the water. "Although I don't think *la Princesa* agreed." He said referring to Elena Hernandez the woman Carlos had married when he was still in his twenties. The marriage had only lasted a couple of years.

"No, *la Princesa* was not amused."

"A blue-assed groom wasn't what she was expecting on her wedding night." Diego dead-panned, "Too much tequila and bad things happen." He flipped his brother-in-law a knowing grin.

Pedro was more introverted and less gregarious than Diego, but he had a wicked sense of humour. He was more often the mastermind of their pranks, smiling innocently in the background as Diego implemented the plan.

Close friends since childhood the two men were physically opposites. Diego was tall, muscular and long-legged. He had been told he had an infectious laugh and a mischievous sparkle in his dark eyes, offsetting the menacing appearance of his often-broken nose. Sometimes his medium-length black hair was combed straight back and firmly gelled in place. Today he hadn't applied the glutinous gunk allowing the wind to tousle his unruly mop.

Pedro, on the other hand, was built like his Mayan ancestors with a long, stocky body and shorter legs. He was incredibly strong and had when necessary lifted outboard motors that weighed as much as he did. Pedro's profile could have been the model for the stone carvings at any of the Mayan temples with his blade-shaped nose, deep-set eyes and chiselled lips. He was bald by choice, not genetics.

Nothing had made Diego happier than when Pedro's younger sister, Cristina, had fallen in love with him. She was kind, smart, funny and beautiful, plus she was happy that her brother and her husband were best friends.

Diego sighed with happiness. *Life is short and this is heaven on earth.* His dad had taught him to savour the moment; to enjoy the warmth of the sun, the salty smell of the wind, and the spectacular colours of the Caribbean Sea. Earlier a pod of dolphins had been following, playing in the wake of the boat until they had tired of the fun and presumably gone hunting for lunch.

"You didn't answer the question, are we having a stag for Carlos?" Diego asked, again.

"We're too old for that stupid shit." Pedro said, with a slight shake of his head. "Let's just have a get-together with our ladies. A few drinks. A few laughs. Good food. And lots of embarrassing stories about Carlos."

"Not too many stories, or Yasmin might change her mind." Diego warned. He reached for a bottle of water, taking a long deep drink.

"Speaking of embarrassing stories, do you remember last January when we told Carlos that Elena still had a key to the house?

Diego sputtered the half-swallowed water, spewing some through his nose. "Now, that was funny!" He said, wiping his face with the back of his hand.

"They'd been divorced for years, and the dumb ass never thought to change the locks."

Diego's head rocked-back with raucous laughter. "I thought he was going to mess his pants when we told him she had been poking around inside his house." Still snickering at the memory Diego glanced at the dashboard, checking the autopilot. *Todo bien*. Satisfied, he lifted his gaze hoping to spot a sea turtle or two, or perhaps another pod of dolphins.

"When we told him the look on his face was priceless." Pedro chuckled, "He called the locksmith and had the locks changed, pronto!"

"Elena said she was on the island visiting her mother and wanted to say hello to Carlos, but couldn't find him. And we couldn't tell her he'd been kidnapped." Diego felt a wave of uneasiness sweep over him, his laughter died. "That could have ended tragically for both Carlos and my son José." He said, remembering how his impetuous son had secretly followed him on their search for Carlos. He whispered *Gracias a Dios* as he sketched the sign of the cross.

"Yes, it could have," Both men were silent for a few minutes, then Pedro said, "We should head back. I promised Maricruz I'd take her out for dinner tonight."

"You two are getting pretty serious," Diego said, as he tapped the throttles and increased their speed. Diego liked and respected Teniente Maricruz Zapata, and hoped her relationship with Pedro would continue to thrive. He was a good man who wanted someone to love and to be loved.

She was beautiful and fit, and she was a very capable lieutenant in the Mexican Navy. The three of them had met during the aftermath of Hurricane Pablo but Pedro and Maricruz had gotten off to a wobbly start. She had not been impressed with his chauvinistic quips.

It was during the recovery operation of a murdered local man that Maricruz finally understood the problem. Pedro was as skittish as a teenager with a crush. He didn't know how to have just an ordinary conversation with a *female* lieutenant. She reluctantly agreed to meet him for a coffee. Over a long and progressively more relaxed conversation she discovered they shared a fascination with the ocean, a desire to travel, a love of good food, and a wacky sense of humour.

She had later told Diego that she now thought Pedro's initial awkwardness was quite cute.

Diego had snorted with laughter. Pedro. Cute. That was like saying a full-grown Brahman bull was cute.

Chapter 6

October 15th Cancun

"Pastel pink! You want me to wear baby girl pink?" Jessica asked, holding a floor-length fluffy confection under her chin. The colour was so pale she looked like a ghost. Her wishy-washy image was infinitely reflected by the mirrored walls of the elaborate dressing room. This was the tenth or maybe the eleventh Cancun bridal store they had visited in the last month. Every spare hour when they weren't working at the restaurant, was consumed with planning *the wedding* which was rapidly becoming *the* social event of the year, she mused as she mentally made air quotes. In her limited experience it was a common trait among brides, fretting over little details but not actually making any definite decisions until pushed.

"It was just a suggestion," Yasmin snapped, as she slumped down onto a padded bench.

"It's a horrible suggestion!" Jessica said. She blew out a huff of air, pushing her long bangs off her forehead. "God, it's hot in this store."

"This store is fully air conditioned." The saleswoman standing rigidly behind Yasmin stated. In her arms was yet another over-the-top pile of lace and sparkly geegaws.

"Jess, you are being difficult." Yasmin added.

"Me ... being difficult?" Jessica said, her voice raising a little at the end. "We've been traipsing all over Cancun in and out of every bridal store. First this dress, then that dress. With a long train. Without a long train. Lace and then no-lace. Seductive and then demure. With lots of shiny crap sewn on, or plain and simple. I am surprised we haven't flown to Mexico City to check the thousands of bridal stores there."

"You're my best friend, and my maid-of-honour. You're supposed to be supportive." Yasmin chided.

Jessica thrust the offending gown at the saleswoman, who deftly placed it on top of one she was holding. Jessica flopped onto the bench beside Yasmin. "Yassy, I'm sorry." She put her arm around her. "I'm trying to be supportive, I'm just tired of looking at all of these ...," She flung her arm up, and with difficulty curbed her desire to curse crudely, "... dresses."

"I know. I know. But, I can't order invitations, or pick the linens, or choose my flowers until we decide on the colour scheme. The bridesmaids' dresses are important!"

"Yes, they are, but shouldn't we just concentrate on one thing at a time? What type of dress you want to wear?"

Yasmin's eyes shone with unshed tears. "Perfect. I just want it to be perfect."

"That's easy. Whatever dress you wear will be perfect, and you will be breathtakingly beautiful." Jessica stood up and held her hand out to Yasmin. "Come on, let's take a break. We'll go have a late lunch somewhere really expensive, drink a bottle of wine or maybe even a bottle of champagne. We'll get tipsy and celebrate your happiness."

"You have to help me find a dress. I couldn't bear doing this with my mom's helpful suggestions." Yasmin pleaded, making air quotes with her fingers when she said the words 'helpful suggestions.'

Jessica sputtered a laugh, "Of course I will. I love your mom, but she can be a nightmare when she's on a mission."

"I know! Help me, please."

"Food and wine now, then we'll try again another day, okay?"

Yasmin turned to the saleswoman who had patiently been bringing dress after dress for them to try on. "Muchas gracias Señora, but we didn't find what we are looking for."

Jessica caught the flash of exasperation in the woman's eyes as she murmured "De nada" and dipped her chin disdainfully acknowledging Yasmin's thanks.

"Would the Señoritas like me to radio for a taxi?" The uniformed doorman asked politely.

"Si, gracias."

The man stepped outside and used a handheld transmitter to contact one of the Taxi Naranja fleet, catering specifically to solitary female passengers.

Jessica knew the fare would be more costly, but the cars were always air-conditioned, newer and definitely cleaner than the taxis that roved the streets of Cancun. Personally she had no problem with stepping out on the curb and raising her hand to signal a taxi that she wanted a ride, but she wasn't completely oblivious to her vulnerability as a woman on her own. She would make it obvious to the driver as she noted the vehicle number and then sent a brief text to Yasmin or Diego, just in case.

There had been a few incidents of solitary female being attacked by a male driver, usually late at night and after the woman had been out for a few drinks with friends. In this case, a short ride to the new shopping mall wouldn't cost that much more, and an air-conditioned taxi would be a treat.

Five minutes later the doorman opened the heavy glass entrance door and said, "Your car is here. Allow me." Then he opened the rear door on the taxi to allow Jessica and Yasmin to enter.

Jessica raised her eyebrows when Yasmin slipped a hundred pesos into his hand as a tip for arranging the taxi.

"My mother would have been indignant at our behaviour." Was her only explanation.

"Really? You only said we couldn't find anything we liked."

"We argued in front of a salesperson. In my mother's world you disagree, privately."

Jessica smiled to herself. Yasmin came from an old and comfortably well-off family. The Spanish surname of Medina, derived from the ancient Arabic word for city, had been in Mexico since at least the 1520's. Moneyed Mexican families behaved like wealthy European families. It was all about perception. Jessica's family had been in Canada since the 1720's but were from poor Scottish and Irish immigrants who were searching for a better life in a new country. Her family was raucous, silly, and frequently loud.

"A dondé vas? Where are you going?" Asked the taxi driver.

"The shopping mall in Puerto Cancun. There are some fabulous restaurants there." Jessica replied.

The taxi driver glanced once over his left shoulder then accelerated rapidly into a small gap in the crush of rushing vehicles.

The taxi driver's quick maneuver brought a grin to Jessica's face. The first time she had driven a car in Mexico, it had been an eye-opening experience. Moving from her home in Canada to Isla Mujeres with friends, she had driven most of the eight-thousand five-hundred kilometers. She preferred being the driver. As a passenger the movement of the vehicle would lull her to sleep and she'd miss the adventure of the road trip.

In Mexico the drivers zigged and zagged between lanes, zipping into any available gap with or without signaling. Passing on corners or on hills was normal. If you turned on your left indicator it could mean one of two things; either it's safe to pass me, or I'm turning left. Accidents were rare, but often deadly as most cars were not equipped with airbags or had seatbelts that functioned.

Jessica's stomach rumbled noisily, "I'm starving. What do you want to have for lunch?"

"Fish," Yasmin answered, "Fresh grilled grouper would be perfect."

Neither woman noticed as two car lengths back a rust-spotted white delivery van smoothly pulled away from the curb and followed the taxi.

~

Yasmin and Jessica relaxed with a second glass of a full-bodied Argentinean Malbec. "Oh my god, that was an amazing meal." Jessica said.

"My grilled fish was perfect." Yasmin agreed. She contemplated the dessert menu strategically placed when their server had refilled their wine glasses. *My favourite, dark-chocolate mousse.* She reluctantly closed the menu, she couldn't stuff another morsel into her stomach. "I still don't have a clue what to do for my colour scheme. Do you?" She asked.

Jessica leaned back in the padded chair and fanned her arm in a semi-circle. "What you see around you Yassy."

Intrigued Yasmin allowed herself to slowly take in their surroundings. "Flowers; deep purple, bright red, tropical pink, lemon yellow, and tangerine orange."

"What else?" Jessica prompted.

"The turquoise colour of the ocean, the lime green tropical plants, and the dark green palm fronds."

"Yep, and one more thing ... the sapphire blue sky."

"What are you trying to tell me?"

"You are getting married on a tropical island in the Caribbean Sea. Celebrate your surroundings. Use all the colours that you just mentioned." Jessica could almost see the idea whirling around in Yasmin's head as she thoughtfully surveyed the oceanfront garden.

"Jessica, that's perfect! Every bridesmaid will wear a different colour. The table cloths and napkins, even the flowers can be a rainbow of hues and shades. What a fabulous idea."

"I know, I'm a genius, right?"

"Yes, yes you are!" Yasmin leapt out of her seat to hug Jessica. "An absolute genius."

"And I get first pick of the colour for my dress."

"You are a scheming, conniving genius. And yes, you can choose whatever colour you like."

"No baby girl pink!"

"Deal, no baby girl pink for anyone!

Chapter 7

October 15th Cancun

Fuentes shifted on the worn seat of the plain white, utility van. Something hard pressed on the sciatic nerve, numbing his left butt-cheek. He had parked in the shade of a coco palm with a view of the main entrance of the shopping mall. Finally settled, he lowered the windows hoping for a cooling breeze, but the mid-October air was hot and still, refusing to cooperate.

There were still two more weeks in the official hurricane season and hopefully no other storm would develop. Hurricane Pablo had blasted across the peninsula at the end of August and the municipalities were still clearing up the mess. It would be another few weeks before the temperature dropped into the mid-twenties Celsius.

For this assignment he could have chosen any of the twelve luxury vehicles parked in *Don Rafael's* climate-controlled garage; the all-black Lincoln SUV, or the nimble F-Type Jaguar coupe, or even the staid old-man's Rolls Royce. The fully-loaded white Jeep Sahara was his personal favourite, but today he wanted an un-remarkable vehicle, something so common it wouldn't be noticed. He had decided on the plain-Jane, well-used van then plunked a scuffed tool box on the passenger seat. Dressed in tattered jeans and a stained t-shirt he was just another hardworking man trying to make a living doing small repair jobs.

Fast food wrappers and discarded coffee containers littered the floor. The smell offended him, but it was all part of the disguise should the *policía* take interest in him or the van. He had his seatbelt draped loosely across his lap, like a local would wear it. The majority of Cancun drivers considered it to be too much bother to repeatedly fasten and unfasten the contraption. By pulling it across their chest they hoped it was enough to fool the cops into thinking they were actually using the safety device. If a driver was pulled over it was because the policía wanted a *mordidita*, a little bite, a bribe to ignore the violation.

Glancing at the time on his cellular he noted the women had been inside for over two hours. Shopping or eating, or both. It didn't matter, he was patient. Today's task was surveillance, not the actual mission.

~

Yasmin's cell phone jingled with the ring tone she had assigned to Carlos. "Hola, mi amor." She said.

"Hola carina. Where are you?" His voice purred in her ear.

"Shopping for my dress." She answered pulling a face at Jessica, signalling her to keep quiet.

"Ah, and I hear the clink of cutlery and dishes in the background. Can I assume that you ladies are taking a break, perhaps with a glass of vino or two?"

"Si, we are. At Puerto Cancun," Yasmin said, then mouthed *busted*!" at Jessica. "But it was Jessica's idea." She added.

"Of course, it was." He laughed. "Will you be back on the island *para la cena*, by dinner-time?" He asked, meaning closer to eight or nine in the evening.

"We'll head back as soon we are finished our lunch. Jessica is cranky and needs a nap." She said with a smile quirking the corners of her mouth.

"No, I'm not!" Jessica said raising the volume on her voice and leaning towards Yasmin. "Yasmin is dithering."

Yasmin heard Carlos' rich laugh and she grinned. What an amazing man she was marrying. Kind, generous, a good sense of humour, and extremely sexy.

"Let me know when you are on the Ultramar, I will pick you up at the entrance."

"I'll call to let you know, mi amor, but we won't need a ride. Jessica left her golf cart *Frita Bandidta* in the parking lot. We're fine."

"Okay, carina. Enjoy your lunch."

"Wait!" Jessica yelled, just as Yasmin was about to say goodbye to Carlos. "It's only three in the afternoon. We're already in Cancun, and we now have the beginnings of an idea. Let's give it one more try."

Yasmin gave her a puzzled look, "Really, I thought you were fed up with shopping."

Jessica held up her wine glass, "Motivation! I'm good for another three hours."

"Did you hear that?" Yasmin said to Carlos, "She wants to continue looking for dresses."

"Better her than me." He answered.

"Can you ask him to let Sparky out for a pee?" Jessica said. "He's locked inside my house."

Yasmin handed Jessica the phone, "Here, you ask him."

~

"*Hola jefe.*" Jessica said.

"Hola troublemaker. What can I do for you?" He asked.

"Let Sparky out for a pee, and feed him? Or maybe ask Luis to stop by? He still has a key to my place."

"Really? Luis still has your key even after your, this-is-not-a-permanent-situation, speech over a month ago." He teased, "Interesting, very interesting."

"Hey, that was a private conversation. How did you find out?"

"You were at the *Loco Lobo* when he came to get your key." Carlos replied, "I was standing only few feet behind you, but you were talking loud enough for everyone in the restaurant to overhear your conversation."

"Dammit." She muttered, "I only gave him a key a few hours before Hurricane Pablo arrived so he could check on my dog. If you remember I was helping you get the restaurant secured for the storm." She said, "I just haven't got around to asking for it back, yet."

Laughter was the only response from Carlos.

"It's convenient for times like this." She retorted. "Then I don't have to panic over Sparky needing a pee."

"Convenient. I'll let Luis know you think he's convenient." He was still laughing when he disconnected the call.

"Jerk!" Jessica said to the silent device.

"Hey, that's my man you are calling a jerk." Yasmin said, her smile softening her peeved tone.

"Dammit, he knows how to push my buttons."

"Si, and it amuses him when you react."

Jessica snorted a laugh, "You're right, it does amuse him. Okay, let's pay our bill and get back on the hunt for that perfect dress."

Yasmin turned to look for their waiter, then catching his glance she made a scribbling motion in the air – signalling him to add up their bill. She tipped back the last dribble of the deep-red wine and patted her lips with the linen napkin. "*Muy rico.*"

Once the bill was settled the women exited into the hot afternoon sun, heading towards the mall entrance and the taxi *sito*.

Sliding across the back seat of the taxi, Jessica said to Yasmin, "Do you still have that list of all the bridal shops in Cancun?"

"Si," She replied pulling a crumpled piece of paper out from the depths of her large shoulder bag. "We've been to most of them already."

"We haven't tried that one." Jessica said pointing at the last name on the list the Barzené Boutique on Bonampak.

"It's not technically a bridal shop, but I have seen the beautiful dresses that are displayed in the street-front windows." She shrugged, "sure, it's our last option. Let's try it."

"Or we could go to Mérida next weekend and try the stores there." Jessica suggested with a wry grin.

"Mérida, and my mother's delightful suggestions." Yasmin shook her head, "I would look like Queen Isabella of Castile by the time she finished with me." Yasmin leaned forward and said to the driver. "Barzené por favor."

~

As the taxi pulled away from the entrance, the battered dirty white van slid in behind it, keeping a couple of vehicle lengths back. Fuentes briefly thought about his full bladder and decided that if they went into another store he would find a café or bar and take a quick piss and buy a bottle of water to quench his thirst.

It amazed him how many hours women could spend shopping. He preferred to go into one store, pick out five or six shirts, two pairs of pants, a package or two of underwear, pay for his purchases and leave. He might spend an hour or two in total buying sufficient clothing to last him a year.

So far neither of the women were carrying bags to indicate that they had made any purchases. Although, he supposed, fancy bridal gowns and bridesmaids' dresses would need to be specially ordered and picked up closer to the actual date. He didn't have any experience with the process other than observing other people's lives.

He was by necessity still single. A wife and children were a weakness that would be exploited by his enemies. His phone rang just as he had parked the van within sight of yet another high-end dress store.

"Bueno?" He answered.

"Where are you?" Fernandez demanded.

"Avenida Bonampak." Fuentes answered cryptically, knowing that cellphones could be tapped.

"I need you back here, now."

"Claro, veinte minutos jefe." He had no idea what was so urgent, but when the *Don* said now, he meant immediately. The heavier afternoon mash of vehicles would slow him down but he knew shortcuts that would get him back to *Don* Rafael's compound quickly. Relieving his bladder would have to wait.

Chapter 8

October 30th Just after midnight

Jessica maneuvered her ten-year-old golf cart *Frita Bandidta* into the tight parking space outside her casa. At twenty minutes past midnight the sight of her the little house glowing brightly under the street lights made her smile. The owners had painted it a cheery Caribbean combination of hues; orange walls, and pink window frames and a glossy turquoise door. Inside was another wild combination of hues. To her Mexico was colour, lots of colour that's why she loved living in the *colonias.*

But parking in her neighbourhood was a problem. The area was affordable because the living spaces were tiny multi-family dwellings, crammed side-by-side, plus frequently two or more apartments would be situated at the front and the back of a skinny strip of property with a narrow pathway servicing both dwellings. The streets were jammed with a proliferation of motos, cars, trucks, and more recently privately owned golf carts.

Some nights her neighbours, on either side of her casa, left her so little room to park she had to man-handle the motos back or forward a few inches then jockey her *carito* into whatever space was available. Nobody got upset, it was just the way it was.

She unlocked the front door and was enthusiastically greeted by Sparky. He put his wide front feet on her knees as she bent to hug his compact but muscular body. "How's my boy? You miss me, sweetie?" She asked as his tail swished rapidly back and forth. He was a quiet dog, and only barked when he was warning her of danger, or in the rare instance when she was taking too long to organize herself before taking him for a cart ride. Then, he would give her one loud hurry-the-hell-up *woof!*

She smooched him on his nose and released him, "Come on boy, time for pees and poops before bed." Jessica turned and secured the front door then crossed through the kitchen to her back door. She opened it allowing Sparky access to her miniscule back yard. "Hurry up, the bugs are ravenous tonight."

She had been told by locals not to install a pet door for Sparky. It would just be another way that someone could, or at least would try, to get into her house to steal electronics or cash. It was a bloody nuisance, but it was the modern-day reality even in her relatively-crime-free home town in Canada. Pet doors for tiny dogs, or cats still worked, but for a pooch with Sparky's broad shoulders a small child could squeeze through and then open the door for the adult instigator waiting outside.

Sparky sauntered inside, and settled in his bed watching Jessica. Just as she was about to strip down and hop in the shower, Jessica heard what sounded like a large piece of hard plastic hitting the pavement. Sparky stood and faced the front door. He woofed, only once, but loudly. Curious she picked up her heavy police baton-style flashlight and pulled opened the front door.

Sparky woofed louder and shouldered past her legs, into the street.

"Shit!" She yelled, as she spotted the siphon hose spewing fuel from her gas tank onto the street. Beside her cart was a plastic container, three-quarters full of gasoline. She snatched up the siphon hose ensuring the remaining contents drained into the tank.

"Bloody *pinche pendejo bandido*!" She cursed loudly, knowing that the person was likely standing a few feet away waiting to see what she would do next. She screwed the top on the plastic carboy and dragged the heavy container inside her front door. The plastic jug reeked of slopped gasoline and it wasn't a great idea to stash it inside her home but she was spitting mad and sure as hell wasn't letting that pilfering *pendejo* get his hands on her gas.

Theft of golf cart batteries, fuel, and even seats was a big problem on the island. Over time most locals had retrofitted their carts with a metal hasp and strong lock to keep the front seat from being lifted.

With Sparky trailing at her heels she returned to her vehicle and replaced the gas tank cap, plus what had been until tonight her inexpensive, but theft-proof accessory. One of her Canadian friends had suggested the simple add-on. It was a piece of plastic drainage pipe large enough to cover the gas cap, with a PVC cover glued on one end. By locking down the seat, the burglars hadn't been able to access the tank from either the top or from under the vehicle with that simple little trick her friend had taught her.

Tonight however, she realized the *bandido* had used something to pry up the hasp, pulling the screws right out of the wooden seat and had tossed aside her back-up safety feature. That was the sound that she and Sparky had heard. The heavy plastic cap bouncing on the pavement. Not only was he a *pendejo*, he was an *estúpido pendejo*.

Realizing there was quite a bit of gas around and under her cart, she irritably unwound the garden hose attached to the front of her neighbours' house and spayed down the street and sidewalk. She would explain to Enrique and Rosa tomorrow why she was using their water, and bring them a bottle of wine as a thank you. Water, like electricity was expensive. The main water supply and the electrical conduit ran under the ocean between the mainland and the island. Everything had to be imported – and at great cost.

Stinking of gasoline Jessica headed back to her house, and had the shower she had been about to enjoy when she was interrupted. She slipped on a large soft t-shirt and pair of shorts. If the knucklehead was foolish enough to try again, she planned to be dressed and ready to chase him off. Restless and listening for odd sounds she poured herself a cold Isla Brewing Playa Norte cerveza, and flopped into her favourite chair.

Legs draped over the padded arm of the chair, she allowed herself a few minutes of mindless social media interaction to quieten her overactive senses while she sipped the beer. She slid a finger over the screen to activate her social media pages.

Jessica stared at the date displayed on her smartphone and shook her head in disbelief. *Had it only been one year?* Only one year since she and Yasmin had begun their sketchy, treasure-hunting adventure? After an evening of consuming too much alcohol, they had jokingly decided to search for the cache rumoured to have been buried on the island in the late 1880's by the pirate Fermin Antonio Mundaca.

When they uncovered a letter written by Mundaca to the object of his unrequited love, Martiniana Gomez Pantoja also known as La Trigueña, their efforts intensified. The letter read:

"My dearest sweetheart I am leaving you everything I have in the world, because I love you. When I built the hacienda that I intended to share with you, I uncovered the treasure buried by Captain Lorencillo de Graaf. I have been told de Graaf was the Dutchman who in 1683 raided the rich Spanish stronghold of Veracruz. I have moved the valuables to a safer place and this letter will help you find the location. This is what I give to you. I will love you forever, Fermin Mundaca."

Several weeks later all they had to show for their efforts were threats of imprisonment, an attempt on Yasmin's life and thousands — or perhaps millions — of mosquito bites. The one good thing from the entire episode had been the discovery of Sparky. He had been a skinny stray, covered in fleas and ticks and shaking with fear when she found him hiding in the woods. What a little gem he had turned out to be.

She had recently rescued another terrier-mix mutt the day Hurricane Pablo battered the island. When the hurricane had moved on and she cautiously cracked open her front door she had found a moaning bundle of filthy fur huddled against on her doorstep. When she managed to get him into the local veterinary clinic, Dr. Delfino discovered the dog had a broken leg, and was undernourished and tick infested.

A few days later one of her friends recognized the dog, and said that he had been surviving on the street for five years. In the neighbourhood where he scrounged food he was known as Max. Several people occasionally left him dry kibble to supplement his garbage-can scavenging, but everyone in the neighbourhood already had two, three or four dogs and no one wanted to officially claim him.

Jessica had let Max recuperate at her house before convincing a friend near Phoenix, Arizona to adopt him. Two energetic dogs were just too much for her to handle and the added cost was killing her limited budget. After five years of near-starvation Max loved to eat. Anything that was being offered, any time of day he was happy to eat.

For the short time Max lived with them Sparky became a little less finicky about his food. Sparky had watched the drool stream from Max's mouth as he waited to hoover up the left-overs. However, now that Sparky was once again the prince of the realm he had reverted to his snobbish attitude. He was smart and manipulative, and she adored his quirky character. When he laid down with a huff, put his head on his paws and stared his plate she was sure he was thinking;

Chicken again? No thank you. I'm in the mood for steak!

Jessica picked up her empty beer bottle, and rinsed it under the tap to ensure there wouldn't be a *cucaracha fiesta* a cockroach party in her kitchen. Those little devils loved adult beverages.

She plugged her iPhone into the charger, and turned out the lights.

Bedtime!

Chapter 9

October 30th Late morning

"Well, damn." Jessica glared malevolently at the heavy container she had dragged back outside to her golf cart. "How the hell am I supposed to refill my tank without slopping gas everywhere?" She checked the time, *Enrique should be up by now. He might have a funnel.*

Rapping lightly on his front door, she hollered, "Hola. Hola Enrique."

A couple of minutes later Enrique pulled the door open. He was wearing a pair of dark blue work shorts, but no shirt. His right hand finger-combed his hair.

"Hola Jessica, ¿Cómo está? He asked, then put his large short-fingered hand over his stretched mouth to cover a yawn. Many of her Maya friends had wide hands, and when compared to her long slim-fingered hands, very short blunt fingers. But, damn those short-fingered hands were strong.

Generations of hard physical work had created tough, resilient people.

"Bien, bien, gracias, Enrique. Tienes ... ummm ... Yo no sé cómo se llama en español ..." She said, trying to illustrate a funnel with her hands. She tried to use her dreadfully basic Spanish whenever possible, but sometimes the words just weren't there.

"No entiendo." He replied with a perplexed smile and rubbed his nose. She could see he hadn't fully woken up yet, and was having trouble figuring out what she wanted.

Jessica pointed at her golf cart. She had unlocked and lifted the front seat out the hinges, then set it on the ground. The previously-theft-proof cap was sitting on the floor along with the regular gas cap. Switching back to English she said, "A funnel. I need to put fuel in my carito."

"*Embudo*!" Then he switched to English which he spoke much better than her disjointed Spanglish. "What happened? Are you out of gas?"

"No, a *pendejo bandido* emptied my tank last night. Sparky and I scared him off. He left behind his jug and siphon hose." She said, grinning at her neighbour.

"Jessica, you should be more careful." He lightly scolded her.

"No worries." She laughed, and shook her head. "Do you have a funnel I could borrow?"

"Si, momentito." He said, holding up his thumb and forefinger a small distance apart. It was a common hand-gesture, meaning *give me a moment, please.* Ten minutes later Enrique returned. He had buttoned a colourful plaid shirt over his short, wide body, and he was holding the top half of a two-litre plastic Coca Cola bottle. The label was still attached to the portion in his hand.

"A Mexican funnel!" He said with a laugh, inverting the neck to demonstrate what he meant.

"Great idea! Why didn't I think of that?"

"Because you don't drink gallons of Coca, like me." He said, patting his ample tummy affectionately.

One corner of her mouth tweaked up in a half-grin. *Why do guys do that?* Over-weight men, the world over, possessively rubbed their large bellies; like a proud parent caressing a beloved child.

Enrique bent and easily lifted the container that she had dragged with difficulty from her house to the sidewalk.

"I'll do it." He said, "Just hold the *embudo* steady for me."

Two minutes later the liquid slopped over the filler and splashed on their feet. He laughed, and pointed at the half-full container. "The *bandido* left more gas behind than he took from you."

"Bonus!" Jessica said, giving him a thumbs-ups.

"Where do you want me to put the container?"

"How about your bodega?" She asked, meaning his storage area. "I don't want it inside my house, again."

"Okay, I'll write your name on the jug so that we remember it's yours."

"Don't be silly, Enrique. If you need it for your moto, use it." She replied, "I only go through one tank of gas in a week."

He grinned and popped one shoulder in a self-conscious shrug, "My moto is empty, and payday isn't until Saturday."

"Then fill it up!" Jessica said, "I'll hold the ... *embudo*. Is that right?"

"Si, correcto."

~

"Okay little buddy," Jessica said to Sparky, "It's time for me to head to work and make us some grocery money." She picked up the keys to her *carito*, patted her bra to be sure her cell phone was securely tucked into the left side, and checked her smile in the hallway mirror. When she was a teenager her parents insisted she wear braces and she had a picture-perfect smile, a benefit when working for tips to augment her minimum-wage server's job.

Locking her front door, Jessica turned around and climbed into the passenger side of the cart. She stepped across to the driver's side, avoiding the muddy paw prints left on the seat by Sparky after his morning swim. She stuck the key in the ignition and moved the gear shift from forward to reverse, and pushed down on the gas pedal.

Frita Bandidta hesitated a moment or two as was her habit then she finally cooperated and backed up. Jessica swung the steering wheel to the left, checked for traffic in both directions on the narrow street and eased out of her constricted parking space.

Fifteen minutes later Jessica tucked *Frita Bandidta* in behind the drab Casa de Cultura on the corner of Abasolo and Guerrero Avenues. The building was a gloomy, randomly-maintained municipal property that occasionally presented cultural events.

She didn't like parking behind the poorly lit structure because she typically finished working well after midnight, but parking was practically non-existent in Centro. Many of the homeowners blocked the area in front of their small casas with large buckets filled with rocks or concrete to prevent anyone else from using their spot.

Most nights Yasmin or another server would walk with her to the parking lot and then she would give the person a ride back to their moto, or a ride home. Now that Yasmin and Carlos were engaged they were seldom apart, leaving Jessica to find other people to keep her company. It wasn't that she felt in danger, it was more a preventative measure. A woman walking alone with a pocket full of cash — tips earned working the lucrative afternoon shift in a popular bar — might be considered an easy target.

Chapter 10

October 30th Late afternoon

As she ambled along Avenida Hidalgo Jessica waved hello to friends who worked in the multitude of open-air restaurants and crammed dimly-lit shops lining both sides of the street. Only five blocks long, the street ran in a northerly direction from the square in Centro to the corner of the old original cemetery. Hidalgo was closed to vehicle traffic, except for the random naive tourist driving a golf cart and happily waving back at the gesturing and shouting locals.

The corner of Jessica's mouth tweaked up as she remembered a recent conversation she had overheard between a puzzled driver and his equally baffled passenger.

"What they are saying?"

"It sounds like cerrada or cerrado."

"You sure it's not ho-la?" The driver asked, forcefully pronouncing the silent *h*.

"No, definitely not hola. I know that word."

"Do a Google translation." The driver said, as he dodged around the street-side patrons. "I'm sure they are just saying hello."

Her attention back on her destination she marveled at how much had been accomplished in the two months since Hurricane Pablo had flooded the low-lying streets with a chest-deep slurry of water, seaweed, sand, and dying creatures. Residents, both island-born locals and foreigners had pitched in to clean and repair the damage. People who chose to live on an island were typically resilient and caring people, willing to assist a neighbour at any opportunity.

Tourism was the mainstay of the island economy, and everyone hustled for the vacationers' dollars. By six in the evening the street would be raucous with loud music pouring out of every restaurant, the fire-dancers and drummers drowning out conversations, the mariachis and trinket vendors all hoping to make a few dollars. She had learned to tune out the background pandemonium.

While the island was getting back on its feet, the number of visitors had dropped dramatically and some islanders had resorted to peddling illegal drugs to earn a living. The restaurant area was quickly becoming known as the place to purchase your drug of choice. Shrewd vendors eyed the tourists and if the person had a certain look or gave off a naughty, risk-taker vibe they were frequently offered *weed* or *snow*. Jessica seemed to fit their customer profile, young with tattoos but she didn't do drugs. After several emphatic refusals the vendors had finally got the message and stopped pestering her.

"Hola Yassy," Jessica said, sauntering into the *Loco Lobo* through the open-air, street-level entrance. "How's it going?"

"Busy!" Yasmin replied.

Jessica checked the clock above the bar, the hands said four in the afternoon, but the background design read, *It's wine o'clock.* Anytime was drink time when people were on holidays.

"I heard from Mom today. Everyone in my family is coming for *the* wedding." Jessica said, putting special emphasis on *the*. She had teased Carlos a few times that the event was a cross between a royal marriage and a rock-star performance. He had good-naturedly rolled his eyes and agreed.

Yasmin and Carlos were popular, both as individuals and as a couple. The guest list currently included two hundred and fifty people, with more being added as friends reminded them not to forget this person or that person.

Jessica added. "Even my Auntie Pattie is coming. She was able to get time off from her job." Jessica lifted her small black apron off the hook and wrapped it around her hips, securing it with a neat bow as she talked.

"Terrific! Where does she work?"

"She's a nurse just like my mom, but at a different facility." Jessica said, "Although she originally went to university in California at Berkley."

Yasmin flicked a perplexed glance at her, "Why would she go to university so far from home?"

"I don't know. The experience maybe?" Jessica popped her shoulders in a quick shrug, "I never actually asked. I was more interested in why she was an Ohio state football fan. She follows the Ohio Buckeyes."

"Don't bother explaining that to me. I don't like American-style football." Yasmin retorted. "Americans and Canadians insist on incorrectly referring to our national sport as *soccer*. We, and the rest of the world, call it football."

Jessica suppressed a grin and stayed quiet. Yassy could get quite testy over what she perceived as cultural slights.

"Anyway, I really am excited your family is coming." Yasmin added. Her hands never stopped moving while she talked. She was the fastest, most efficient bartender that Jessica had ever worked with. Even when things were crazy busy, Yasmin was cool and organized.

On the other hand, dealing with the myriad of decisions for *the* wedding could send her into a complete meltdown. Jessica had on several occasions been the calming influence and had gently pushed Yassy into making a choice. So far they had managed to maintain the multi-coloured tropical theme in all of their decisions. They had picked out the table linens, the bridesmaids' dresses and bouquets, Yasmin's bouquet, plus the flowers and decorations for both the church and the reception venue. The invitations had been ordered and were due to arrive from the printers any day now. However, Yasmin's vision of the perfect dress was still eluding them.

It would be ten times cheaper, and a whole lot simpler, for Carlos and Yasmin to elope to a remote island like Bora Bora in French Polynesia, Jessica thought, not for the first time. A simple civil ceremony on the beach with two witnesses and a toes-in-the-sand romantic dinner was her idea of a perfect celebration. *Oh, well. Not her circus, not her monkeys.*

Jessica quickly read the orders for the six drinks that the departing server had yet to deliver. "When is Carlos going to replace his beloved Porsche?" She asked.

"I'm not sure." Yasmin answered. "We've been using my Italika moto to get around and Pedro's Nissan truck for fetching restaurant supplies."

"Is Carlos having trouble collecting on the insurance payout?" Jessica asked.

"No, I don't think so." Yasmin said, "He said we should wait a bit to replace it." To Jessica, Yasmin's answer sounded perplexed.

"It's been over two months now since it was crushed in the storm." Jessica said as she loaded drinks onto a serving tray. "I thought he would have got a new one as soon as the money came through."

"Me too. I'm not sure why he hasn't bought a new car." She said, tilting her eyes up to catch Jessica's. "Then he recently took me out for a nice romantic dinner and during our conversation he kept talking about Diego and Cristina's kids. How funny and sweet they are." She said, "I know he likes them, but he seldom talks about them."

Jessica grinned, "Um, Yassy, he's trying to find out if you want to have a family, without actually coming out and asking you." She chuckled, "He probably doesn't know himself which answer he wants: yes or no."

Yasmin flicked her head up and stared at Jessica. "You really think that's what he was asking?"

"Yes, most definitely. So, what's the answer?"

Chapter 11

December 15th Cancun

With a pair of high-powered binoculars Fuentes secretively watched the long-based reefer truck pull out of the storage facility. No one working at the warehouse, neither the truck driver nor even the depot manager knew his real name or what he looked like. He was simply a recognizable voice, calling from an unidentifiable and disposable number.

Fuentes was not a stupid man, every shipment was a risk. Their well-paid American border guard had been shown videos of what had happened to his recently deceased, over-talkative co-worker and his family. If their agent so much as dripped one drop of nervous sweat on their paperwork he would receive a late-night visit from the *Don*'s crew.

This truck had a sound-proofed section scarcely able to hold the recent batch of imports, a few bottles of water and a bucket for a toilet. The larger part of the shipment was fresh produce headed to the grocery stores, the small portion was people. Many impoverished workers were illegally brought to the United States on a promise of a better life or an education. Once inside the border they would be forced to work as unpaid labourers in agriculture, the garment industry, commercial fishing, domestic workers, or prostitution. Undocumented and held captive by armed guards at the end of the work day they were unable to ask the authorities for help.

The twenty thousand employees of ICE, the US Immigration and Customs Enforcement, were usually one step behind the newest method of transporting people, but there was always a risk. At worst *Don* Rafael would lose money from the seized shipment. They had ensured the trail back to either Fernandez or himself was convoluted and difficult to follow.

It was his habit to study the internet for statistics on human trafficking, searching for information on their competitors. Russia, Slovenia and Venezuela were listed in the top ten, while Mexico hadn't even made the list. Even more intriguing were the states that dealt with the majority of illegally imported and indentured workers; California, New York, Texas, Louisiana, Tennessee, Florida, Washington, Montana, Minnesota and Mississippi. In the southern states that touched along the Mexican border the bulk of the people were forced to work in agriculture. The more northern states concentrated on mail-order brides, sex workers, domestic workers and children.

There was a big market for their products; people and drugs.

~

"Jessica." Carlos stuck his head out of his office door at the *Loco Lobo* and waved her over.

Jessica swung her head right, then left. Her customers were happily occupied with food, drinks and laughter. She strode towards his office, and smiled at Yassy who was sitting across from Carlos.

Yasmin had one slim leg crossed over the other, her top leg bounced with impatience. Her lips barely cracked a smile, "Hi Jess," she said.

"What's up?" Jessica asked, standing half-in and half-out of the doorway, still keeping an eye on her section.

"Yasmin and I are dead-locked on an important decision. We need a tie-breaker."

Jessica's eyebrows shot up towards her hairline. She glanced to Yasmin, then to Carlos. "If this is something personal I don't want to vote." She said, remembering Yasmin hadn't answered when asked if she wanted a family.

"Personal? No, it's nothing personal," Carlos said, then continued, "I just want your opinion on whether or not the *Loco Lobo* should serve a traditional Gringo-style turkey dinner on Christmas Day."

"Nope! But thick, moist turkey sandwiches on fabulously fresh bread, smothered with lots of butter, mayo, cranberry and stuffing for December 26th has my vote!" She beamed a smile at them.

"What?" Carlos and Yasmin said at the same time.

"Christmas Eve, *Noche Buena*, is an important family night in Mexico. Correct?"

They nodded agreement. Jessica saw their puzzled expressions but she swept on with her explanation.

"The traditional dinner starts after midnight mass, featuring heaps of delicious food including either yummy roasted pork or turkey and served with bubbly adult beverages. After dinner there are tequila-fueled illegal fireworks explosions, which leads to excited kids, barking dogs, yowling cats, and screeching roosters. Nobody gets any sleep. All. Freaking. Night." Jessica said.

"Yes, but ... "

"Momentito, please," Jessica said, "Your staff will be tired, hung-over, and super cranky. The chefs will have to prepare an unfamiliar meal for a group of folks who know *exactly* how the dinner should be prepared and served. And believe me they will tell you in no uncertain terms if you screw it up."

She paused, checking their expressions.

Yasmin was nodding with a little smile on her face. Carlos wasn't convinced, yet.

"Okay, for example, the year I moved to Isla I was invited to an important fundraising event that featured a traditional turkey dinner. The chef thought that because cranberry sauce was red and looked like jam, that he could substitute strawberry jam and everyone would be happy." Jessica laughed at the memory. "No one was happy."

"Wait ... wait. There's more." She said giggling.

"A year later two friends were asked to organize a Thanksgiving dinner at a local hotel. They taught the chef how to cook the birds, prepare mashed potatoes, sweet potatoes, plus the typical peas, carrots and cauliflower. They showed the kitchen staff how to plate the meal, and the demonstrated to the waiters how to position the plate with the turkey meat closest to the guest." She shrugged, "Okay, any server should know that's the correct way to place a meal, the meat closest to the customer to make it easier for cutting."

"Anyway," Now she was laughing so hard she had tears in her eyes, "The day before the event they decided they needed more birds. The manager of the hotel went into Cancun and purchased two smoked turkeys. Not fresh! Smoked, because that was all he could find."

She wiped away the tears, "It's impossible to substitute roasted fowl with smoked. The chefs had to slim down the portions to serve everyone. I have no idea what happened to the two smoked birds."

Carlos and Yasmin chuckled at Jessica's stories but she could see Carlos was still skeptical.

"I still don't understand the sandwich idea." He said. He leaned back in his chair and crossed one ankle over the opposite knee.

Jessica quickly checked her section. She really should be out on the floor looking after her customers. She said, "give me two minutes," and raced over to Letty. "I'm just with the boss for a few more minutes. Could you look after my section, please?" She asked.

Letty nodded, "Si, of course." Her co-worker willingly agreed.

Jessica dashed back to the office.

"A turkey sandwich the day after Christmas is my favourite treat." She said, running her tongue over her lips. "The secret for great sandwiches is fresh bread, brown or white, it doesn't matter. Just to-die-for-fresh bread. Plus butter, mayo, cranberry sauce and stuffing."

His eyebrows scrunched together, Carlos asked, "Correct me if I'm wrong, but isn't the stuffing made from bits of bread and savoury herbs."

"Yes," replied Jessica.

"Then why would you put bits of bread between two slices of bread?"

"Why do you crumble up pieces of deep-fried pork skin and sprinkle them on top of your pork tacos?" Jessica countered.

"Because it tastes good. And that's the traditional way to eat pork tacos."

"Same answer!"

Carlos laughed. "Okay, I get it."

"Is that all we would offer?" Asked Yasmin.

"No, we could still offer a limited menu or our regular menu if you want but the hit of the day will be the sandwiches," Jessica said, "And our special drink could be either Cranberry Margaritas, or Candy Cane Martinis."

Carlos dropped his foot to the floor, leaned forward and propped elbows on the desk, "You agree with Jess, Yassy?"

"Si, it sounds like fun." She said, smiling.

"Then that's what we will do."

"Great." Jessica said, turning to leave.

"Wait, one more question."

"Yeah?" She stopped and half-turned to look at Carlos.

"Why did you think we were going to ask you to be the tie-breaker for a personal question?"

She flicked a quick glance at Yasmin's wide-eyed expression, and noticed a miniscule head shake. *They hadn't discussed kids, yet.* Jessica felt the heat rising from her chest to her face. "Um, I ... have no idea." She flicked her head sideways, "Someone is signalling for their bill, gotta go."

As she darted back to her section she heard Carlos ask Yasmin. "Do you have any idea what that was about?"

Yasmin replied, "Look at the time. I'm twenty minutes late relieving Isabela." She blew him a kiss, "Love you!" then quickly followed Jessica out of his office.

Jessica checked on each guest, making note of drinks that needing refreshing, and picking up empty plates. As she handed an order slip across the bar to Yasmin, she muttered. "Yassy, just talk to him. I almost stuck my foot in the poop that time."

"I will. I promise."

"When?"

"Soon," Yasmin replied.

Chapter 12

January 22nd Isla Mujeres

"Oh no! Yasmin yelped, startling Carlos out of his extraordinarily erotic dream.

"What?" His pulse pounded as he sat up and studied her face. She was staring at her mobile. "Yassy, what's wrong?"

"We only have one month until our big day!" She said. "And we still have so much to do."

Carlos stifled his groan, and flopped down. *Wedding day ...* he couldn't wait for the whole damn Hollywood production to be over and done. He had been having an erotic dream about Yasmin when her shout startled him awake. He rolled towards her, thinking maybe they could re-enact his dream.

He reached for her with a seductive smile on his face, the one she could never resist.

She lightly shoved at his chest, "Not now, sweetie. We have things to do." She swung her feet onto the floor and pulled on one of his old t-shirts, hiding her magnificent body.

His erection wilted. Apparently she had learned to resist his suggestive smile. He laid back on his pillow with his head propped in his hands. Thirty freaking more days of planning, and worrying, and fretting. He'd get more action if he joined the monastery.

"Honey?"

"Si, carina?" He said, calling her sweetheart.

"Can you come out here please? I need your advice on something."

Now what? "Be right there." He responded, hoping she wouldn't notice the exasperation in his voice. He pulled on a pair of briefs and then his shorts. He slapped barefoot out to the kitchen, flicking on his expresso machine as he passed by. He had the feeling he was going to need caffeine this morning, lots of caffeine. He bent to kiss the top of her head, glancing down at her iPad. It was opened to a webpage with hundreds of photos. The title read, *34 Things That Will Make You Say, I wish I did that at my wedding.* With a sinking feeling in his gut he asked, "What can I help you with, carina?"

"I found this real cool page on Pinterest, with amazing ideas for ramping up the fun-factor of our reception." She said, her face glowing with excitement. "I want your opinion on a few of these."

"I'd be delighted to but, may I make our coffees first?"

"What?" Yasmin glanced up.

Carlos popped his eyebrows up in a question and pointed at the espresso machine. "Coffee?"

"Si, mi amor. Gracias."

Five minutes later Carlos tossed back a shot of strong espresso, hot enough to blister the roof of his mouth. He didn't care. He needed the caffeine, now. Then he fixed two larger coffees with hot foamed milk and a drizzle of caramel sauce on top.

He set hers beside her elbow, "There you go, mi amor. Just the way you like it." Yasmin had recently decided she preferred what he referred to as *frilly* coffee, a large caramel macchiato. He had adapted to her preferences. It was easier.

Carlos pulled out a chair and sat beside Yasmin then took a slurp of his beverage. *Mierda!* His mouth still hurt from the hot espresso he had gulped, but he had a feeling this was just the beginning of a very long and painful day. He couldn't even use the excuse of needing to check on the restaurant. He had already told her he had the entire day off. He had planned on a long lazy day of sex, food, a bottle of good champagne with more sex and eventually a late dinner. Wedding planning had not even flickered through his lustful thoughts.

"These are some of the ideas that I really like," She said, pointing at a set of two cutesy signs designed to sit on every dining table. Five things his side should know about her. Five things her side should know about him. And a list of funny personality quirks listed underneath.

Oh, please, just shoot me now. Diego and Pedro would piss themselves with laughter over that one!

"I really like this idea too." She said. It was a photo of a framed picture. 'Instagram our special day. Use hashtag #insertnames55543.'

Okay, that one was reasonably harmless. Unless of course, the photos were still being posted after the late-night dinner and the traditional pouring of tequila down the throat of the groom; as much tequila as the man could swallow without instantly puking it up.

"And this one too. We would frame photos of us at different ages to correspond with the number on the guest table." She said, pointing at a picture of a good-looking football hero and a pretty cheerleader-type female at the supposed age of 16, and the big number 16 printed at the top of the frame. "Isn't that a cute idea?"

Oh hell no! I looked like an acne covered wanna-be-gangsta when I was a teenager.

Carlos contemplated the photos while he quietly sipped his coffee. He was stalling for time, time to come up with an acceptable answer; one that wouldn't result in him sleeping alone on his black leather couch for the next thirty days.

"What do you think?" She asked, when he didn't respond.

Avoiding her scrutiny he concentrated on carefully setting his cup down. How could an intelligent, competent, level-headed woman turn into a giggly-schoolgirl when organizing *una boda*? It was beyond him.

"Carlos? What do you think?" Yasmin repeated. He snuck a peek. She snagged his furtive glance with her beautiful deep-green eyes.

"*Carina*, you and Jessica are so much better at making these decisions. Why don't you ask her advice?" He said, feeling a little guilty that he had just thrown Jessica under the bus.

A couple of months ago at the end of a long and busy night at the restaurant, he had suggested Jessica stay for a few minutes and have a beer with him before heading home. They liked and respected each other, but recently hadn't had time to just sit and chat.

Sipping on her second *cerveza*, Jessica had confided that she despised working on all the *girlie* details. She thought he and Yasmin should hop on a jet, go someplace romantic, and just get married.

"Amen to that sister," Carlos had agreed whole-heartedly clinking the top of his beer bottle against Jessica's. They pinkie-swore, to never, ever tell Yasmin, well, until at least their twenty-fifth anniversary celebration, Carlos had added with a mischievous grin.

Now, faced with her determination that he offer opinions on her suggestions Carlos took Yasmin's right hand in both of his, "Carina, I am hopeless. I live in a boring man-cave," he said and waved an arm to indicate his favourite black, white, and grey colour scheme; one which would change after the wedding when Yasmin moved the remainder of her possessions from her rental home near Jessica's. She had wanted to keep up the appearance of living separately, primarily for her very traditional papa.

Making puppy-dog eyes he asked, "How can I possibly be any assistance creating such a beautiful and complex event?"

"But, it's not fair that I make all the decisions. It's your day too." She protested.

"Yes, it is. And I can hardly wait to marry you." He agreed. "But everyone knows it's the bride's special day. The groom is just the nervous dude in the ill-fitting rental tux, who is waiting for the most beautiful woman in the world to walk up the aisle." He held her close, "Please mi amor. Make this a joyous and beautiful event. Do it for both of us."

Yasmin's eyes sparkled with unshed tears. She kissed him passionately, then said, "Si, I will make this an unforgettable day."

While still embracing Yasmin, Carlos' eyes flicked upwards. His lips mouthed, *Gracias Dios! I owe you. Mucho, mucho!*

Chapter 13

February 7th Yucatán channel Isla Mujeres

Pounding hard over the dark ocean, the long thin, *go-fast* boat was practically invisible on radar. The all-fiberglass hull was the state-of-the-art design favoured by traffickers operating in the Caribbean Sea. Without warning the four 200-horsepower Yamaha outboard motors wailed and the craft lurched to a stop. The deckhand stumbled, grabbing a railing for support.

Alejandro Sánchez instinctively shut down the motors, angrily muttering every profanity that came to mind.

High-pitched screaming erupted from the galley.

Sánchez stuck his head below the deck and hissed at the teenagers, "Shut up!" The interior was windowless and furnished with a plain bench, on both sides of the hull. The craft was designed for carrying large amounts of drugs not for passenger comfort. Unable to see where they were going, many of them were sea-sick, weeping, and shaking with fear. His boat reeked of puke.

Madre de Dios, he hated this job.

"*Tio*! What's happened?" Ruben Pech asked. "Did that Cuban *pendejo* sell us bad gas?"

"No. We've hit something." Alejandro retorted. He rubbed his ribs where his chest had smacked into the steering wheel.

"What do we do now?" Sánchez could hear the near-panic in his nephew's voice.

"We try to fix the problem!" Alejandro glared at his eighteen-year-old nephew, and felt his frustration bubble up. "Check below for water leaks." He snapped.

"Claro, *Tio*." Ruben said, scrambling to do as he was told.

Sánchez had been operating boats since he was fourteen, and had little patience with novices. His former deckhand had saved enough cash and recently bought his own vessel, leaving him shorthanded.

This was Ruben's first time on a Cuban job, and his inexperience was potentially dangerous. He barely knew how to use the pistol tucked into the small of his back. The thought of the kid pointing it at someone with the intent to kill was laughable.

The only reason Sánchez had agreed to hire the eighteen-year-old was to help out his younger sister. Her useless husband had moved to Veracruz with a new woman. He had left her with six young children and no money.

Alejandro had been running without navigational lights, but now he needed light to investigate the problem. First he tilted up the motors, lifting the propellers out of the water so he could look for damage. Reaching for his flashlight, he adjusted the beam to its narrowest illumination and shone it on the motors. A mess of dark green cords were wound around three of the motors. One was missing the propeller, entirely. "*Madre de Dios, Fishing nets!*"

"No leaks that I can see, *Tio*," Ruben said cheerfully as he reappeared.

Sánchez flicked a quick glance at his nephew's puppy-dog grin. He looked as if he was waiting for his uncle to pat him, to tell him he was *such a good boy.*

"Don't just stand there." Sánchez pointed at the fouled propellers. "Start cutting and make sure you toss the debris on the deck, not back in the water. I have a call to make." He said.

With a hurt look on his face, Ruben stuck his hand deep into his side pocket and pulled out his folding knife. Carefully pulling open the wicked-sharp blade, he braced his legs, leaned over the transom, and started sawing on the nearest piece of tough polyethylene netting.

Keeping an eye on his nephew's efforts Sánchez keyed the radio, "Casa Grande this is the Musician," He said referring to his free-time diversion as member of a popular mariachi band.

"Musician this is Casa Grande."

"We're delayed arriving to the fiesta this evening."

"How late?"

"Two hours minimum, maybe more."

"The host will be very unhappy."

"Si, Claro. We will compensate with additional time, at no cost." He said, meaning he would renegotiate his price with *Don* Rafael. The delay wasn't Alejandro's fault, but the *jefe* would blame him anyway.

"Keep us informed." Came the curt response.

"Si, I will." He responded to dead air.

He eyed the meagre progress that his nephew had made sawing through the tough cords. It would be quicker if Ruben was in the water cutting the larger pieces free, but there could be sharp-toothed predators feeding on the fish caught in the netting.

Without the motors to keep them moving forward, the craft was lolling from side to side in the swells. Sánchez was fine, but he could see the kid was going to be sick.

"Puke over the side!" He ordered.

Ruben bent over the side and noisily added more bait for the sharks.

An hour later the two sweat-soaked men had finally removed the last of the tough webbing and now Sánchez could properly assess the damage to his motors. The far portside motor was useless. The shear pin must have broken allowing the propeller to twirl off the engine shaft and sink to the seabed below. He carefully lowered the far starboard engine. It started. Good! He let the motor idle while he examined the two that still had blades. He lowered the second motor, and hit start. The engine revved up, but the prop didn't move. Alejandro crossed himself, kissed his closed fist, and tried the third motor. Nothing. He stared at the four expensive Yamaha motors — only one of the son-of-a-bitches was operating properly.

It was going to be a long, slow journey to Cancun. With a heavy sigh, he picked up the radio microphone. It was time to update Fuentes. Maybe he could send out another boat to tow them back. No, that would noticeable and the Coast Guard or the Navy would investigate. *Christ, what a mess.*

~

The recent radio update to Fuentes had not gone well at all. Alejandro knew the *Don* would be livid at the delay. His empire depended on timely deliveries. Drugs or people it didn't matter — the product had to be delivered when promised.

Keeping with the musical theme, used to disguise their conversations, Sánchez had explained that he had a serious failure with three of his instruments. He said he would need to take the instruments to a nearby repair shop, and would contact Casa Grande tomorrow.

Alejandro had made an off-the-cuff comment about women. It was his clue that he would likely limp his craft to la Isla de Mujeres, the Island of Women.

"Si, claro," was all Fuentes responded on the open airwaves.

Sánchez checked his fuel gauge. He should be okay. He'd have to keep an eye on the temperature gauge for the one functioning motor. He slowly aimed towards the Isla Mujeres, heading for one of the small marinas hidden in the Laguna Makax. The operators were savvy enough to not ask awkward questions; questions that could lead to their sudden and unexplained disappearance.

As the dashboard clock display twenty-three hundred hours, eleven at night, Alejandro spotted the marina. Just a few more minutes. Then he had a whole other problem on his hands; what to do with twenty sobbing, smelly females.

Chapter 14

February 7th Isla Mujeres

Inside their small and homey casa, on Isla Mujeres, Diego Avalos slouched in his favourite chair, his long legs stretched in front of him. He smiled at his wife. "Cristina, do you want to walk down to the marina with me?" He asked. "I need a bit of exercise before I go to bed."

She shook her head, "No gracias mi amor." She pointed at her glass of red wine. "I just poured this. It's the first time today I have had five minutes to relax." She cocked an eyebrow at him. "Is that okay?"

"Of course, our ninõs have kept you busy today." He said, referring to their four young children. "Stay and enjoy your vino." He stood, walked towards her, bent his head and kissed her. "Mmmm. Maybe we can do some more of that later?" He hinted.

"Si, it's possible." She teased.

"I won't be long. I'll just check on the *Bruja*, and come back," He said referring to the sport-fishing boat that he co-owned with Cristina's brother Pedro.

"I'll wait up for you." She blew him a kiss, and winked suggestively.

He almost changed his mind, right then. *No, better to let her have her half-hour of relaxation with a glass of wine, then things could get a bit spicy.*

"Back soon, my love." Diego said as he sauntered out into the warm night, and tilted his head back. No moon, no clouds, just stars. Before Cancun became so big, the stars were plentiful and shone like diamonds. Now with all the light pollution from the city, and the increased population on Isla Mujeres only the brightest stars were visible.

At times like this he missed those simpler days, before the internet, before cellphones, and before so many foreigners had discovered his island paradise. But, the foreigners were their best clients for their charters. He couldn't have it both ways he told himself, yet again.

Turning towards the Laguna Makax, a piece of ocean surrounded on three sides by land, he strode towards the small marina where they kept the *Bruja*. Sometimes she was berthed behind the Bally Hoo Restaurante in Centro, and sometimes here. It depended on the frequency of their charters, and if she required maintenance. Both he and Pedro liked having the yacht docked in their neighbourhood when doing repairs. It was easier to run to the local hardware store, or the boat supply place to get the necessary bits and pieces.

Arriving at the marina he keyed open the locked doors, and then pulled them loosely shut behind himself. He walked towards the *Bruja*, intending to check her lines, and give her bow an affectionate pat. It was a superstitious habit that he had picked up from Pedro. A thank-you for their families' good health and good fortune. Pedro was not a religious person, but Diego still held a strong belief in God. Either way, it didn't hurt to tell her that they appreciated her. *She was a female after all,* Diego chuckled to himself, *and it was always a good idea to let the woman in your life know you cherished her.*

As he descended the stairs to the dock his eye caught the dark outline of a boat creeping slowly towards an empty berth. He was about to hail the captain asking if he needed a hand when something stopped him. It was the shape. The craft was long, low and narrow; the design preferred by drug and people traffickers. Diego gradually eased into the thick brush overhanging the stairway.

Maybe he was wrong, but he wasn't about to be a hero until he had a better idea of what this was all about.

He listened as the boat gently nudged against the dock, and the captain shut the motor off. Straining to hear, Diego was certain he was hearing at least two men talking quietly, and perhaps a female or maybe two. The women's questions sounded panicky, afraid.

Diego pulled his iPhone from his pocket, and thought about calling Pedro or Carlos. But why? What made him so uneasy? Sure, they were running without navigational lights and there might be two men plus two or more women on board, but maybe it was nothing more than engine trouble.

Then as the deckhand bent to tie off the steer line, he could see a group of females scrambling off the boat. Two of the women ran straight at the deckhand and stiff-armed him into the water. A hard object landed on the deck as the man tumbled off the wharf. One of the females snatched it up, fumbling to point what looked like a gun at the captain.

"Ayuadame! Ayuadame!" She screamed, Help me! Help me!

Mierda! He rapidly punched Pedro's frequently called number. *Come on, answer.*

"Bueno?" Pedro finally replied.

"This is Diego. There's a problem at the marina. I need help, Navy and police." He hoped Teniente Maricruz Zapata was either sleeping beside him or close by.

"Wait, slow down. What kind of problem?"

"Traffickers! The captives are fighting their way off the boat." He replied, pounding down the dock towards the melee of bodies. "Get me some help! Now."

Five, six or seven terrified females ran past Diego as he hit end call and shoved the phone in his pocket. He didn't have time to count. "Out the gates, and onto the road," He yelled over his shoulder.

Diego slowed, an older man stood beside his vessel calmly pointing a gun at him.

"Stop!" The man said. "This is none of your business." In the time it had taken Diego to call Pedro, the man, likely the captain, had calmly finished securing the lines and was now trying to regain control of the situation.

Diego stopped halfway along the dock, his hands held out by his sides in a non-threatening gesture. He used his chin to point at the woman who was holding the other pistol. "She has a gun."

The other man laughed, "She doesn't have a clue how to use it." Keeping his eyes on Diego he raised his voice, "*Sobrino*, nephew, get your ass out of the water."

"Si, *Tio*," came the meek reply.

"I've already called for help." Diego said. "Why don't you and your nephew just walk away?" His eyes flicked quickly towards the boat. There were still several women inside, likely too petrified to attempt an escape.

"The policía? My employer owns them."

"Not policía, the marinas." Diego replied. He was counting on the captain knowing that the Navy personnel were considered to be honest, unlikely to accept bribes.

Diego watched as he saw the other man's eyes ping towards the roadway. He hoped the man wouldn't call his bluff, and just shoot him. If the bullet didn't kill him, Cristina would. Ever since Jessica Sanderson had adopted her trouble-finding dog Sparky, Diego had been involved one way or another in their escapades. Cristina frequently reminded him, *we have four children and I don't want to be a young widow.* It wasn't always Jessica and Sparky's fault, sometimes trouble just found him. Like now.

Diego tensed as the nephew scrambled onto the dock, a distance away from his uncle. The teenager who had been shakily pointing the gun at the captain appeared to be considering her options; continue to aim at the older man, or maybe at the younger man, or perhaps at him. He really hoped she didn't pick him. The firearm could accidentally discharge, and with his luck the bullet would hit him. And that brought him back to the same dilemma, if the bullet didn't kill him — Cristina would.

"Señorita, put the gun down, or I will shoot you." Demanded the captain.

Weeping the young woman laid the pistol on the wharf and scrambled back to the boat. Ruben snatched it up then pointed it at Diego.

"Take it easy," Diego said, trying to keep everyone calm. "I can see emergency lights headed this way." In his peripheral vision he could see the red, blue and white lights speeding towards the marina. "Please, just go."

"If I leave the shipment behind, I am signing my death warrant with my employer." The man replied.

Diego shrugged, "The way I see it, you are in trouble either way. Some of the women have already escaped. They can describe you, your nephew, and your vessel."

The man seemed to considering Diego's words for a moment then a sly look crossed his face, "Why are you here? Do you own a boat?" He demanded.

"Yes, but I don't have the keys with me. I was only going to check her mooring lines, and then head home." Diego lied. There was no way this bastard was getting the keys to the *Bruja*. He'd jump into the water, and hide under the dock. Not very heroic, but safer.

The captain turned to the younger man, "We have to get off the island however we can, but we can't go home," He said. "If he finds us, we are dead."

Diego was certain the man he was referring to was their employer and obviously not a forgiving man. He also found it interesting the two men had never once used their names when speaking to each other. No matter, the boat would be traceable. The authorities would eventually figure out their names, and maybe, just maybe their boss's name too.

The captain waved his pistol to indicate that the woman and Diego should back up, as he stepped onto the shore. "Don't tempt me, big man," He said.

Chapter 15

February 8th Isla Mujeres

Sleepily Jessica groped for her vibrating phone as it danced a *salsa* across her bedside stand. She checked the call display, *Maricruz. That's odd.*

"Hola Maricruz, que pasa?" She asked, propped on her side with the cell pressed to her ear.

"Hola Jess. Sorry to wake you, but I need a favour."

"At two-thirty in the morning?"

"Si, Diego called out the Navy to help a group of women escaping traffickers. I'm here at the marina where the *Bruja* is berthed."

Jess sat up in bed, now fully awake. "Is Diego okay?"

"Si, he's fine."

"What do you need?"

"Actually, I need Sparky."

"Sparky?" Jessica swung her feet to the floor, and juggled the phone between her ear and shoulder, while pulling on yesterday's shorts. Hearing his name Sparky raised his head, intently watching Jessica.

"He has an excellent nose for finding things. We need him." Replied Maricruz.

"Okay, we can be there in fifteen minutes. But, I thought there were two sniffer dogs based on the island." Jessica bent and grabbed her Skechers. The added support of the shoe would be better than her customary flip-flops. She pocketed her Maglite, a small flashlight with an intensely bright beam.

"Yes, but they are tracking the two men who escaped," Maricruz answered. "I need Sparky to find a group of women who managed to get away."

"If you have two dogs, can't one follow the men and one follow the women?" She couldn't stop pecking questions at Maricruz, while she got ready. She was curious by nature and sucked in information like air.

"Unfortunately the traffickers have split up. The handlers and dogs are following two different scents.

"Okay, got it. We'll be there shortly. Bye."

"Gracias, adios."

With Sparky's eyes following her every move Jessica slipped on a long-sleeved t-shirt. She held one hand towards him in a stop, stay away motion as she sprayed her legs, arms, and neck with her favourite island perfume; Off Insect Repellent. Sparky was allergic to the smell, sneezing dramatically when he caught a whiff but she had to use repellent. The lagoon area was home to millions of hungry mosquitoes, potentially the source of both Dengue and Zika fevers.

"Come on Sparky. We've got work to do." She said, snatching his gear from a hook behind her kitchen door. She held the harness in front of his chest. He stepped into the nylon loops in his customary manner; left foot first, then right foot. She snapped the buckle, attached his lead and he was set to go.

"Keys, phone, two bottles of water, my sunglasses for later, and a water bowl for you." Jessica said, "Okay, we're ready," as she opened the door, then followed her eager canine as he headed straight to the cart.

~

As she drove towards the marina gates, Jessica saw Maricruz helpfully waving her arms overhead. She was difficult to spot wearing her bulky camo uniform. Her slim frame was further disguised by a heavy helmet, a chest-pack covered with pockets, straps and buckles, and thick-soled lace-up boots. Twice, Jessica had attempted to accompany Maricruz on her morning run around the island, but she had rapidly fallen behind. The woman was fit, very fit.

"Hola Jess, thanks for coming." Maricruz said, as Jessica shut off the ignition.

"No worries." She said, "Sparky is happy to lend you a nose."

Maricruz rolled her eyes, at Jessica's lame joke, "Hola Sparky, are you all set?" Maricruz asked, as she affectionately rubbed his ears.

"He's excited, "Jessica said. "Anything that involves a ride and a walk is his idea of a good time." She pocketed keys, stuffed the cellphone in her bra, hooked the sunglasses in the V-neck of her shirt, switched on her flashlight and asked, "Now what?"

"Come with me, I want him to sniff in and around the boat. Hopefully he'll find a scent that he can follow to the road, and then lead us to the women."

"Diego!" Jessica called, momentarily distracted by her tall friend walking towards her. "Are you okay?"

"I'm fine, Jess," He said, as he wrapped her in a big hug.

"Is Pedro here too?"

"Yes," Maricruz answered. "He's working with my crew, searching for the smugglers."

Jessica grinned, "He'd like that, being in on the action." She lightly tugged on Sparky's lead. "So, tell me what happened."

Maricruz pointed at Diego, "It's his story."

"I'm getting tired of repeating myself." He complained. "I've told this story a few times; first to Pedro and Maricruz, then her boss Captain Valentino Dzul and then the crew tracking the bad guys."

"Yeah, yeah." Jessica said, flashing her fingers, "Come on tell me."

Diego sighed, and began again.

"Did you call the policía?" Jessica asked, when he paused for a breath.

"Captain Dzul called it in. Do you remember Sargent Ramirez?" Diego asked.

"Yep, we met after Hurricane Pablo."

"Ramirez and eight constables are searching the boats and marinas at the northern end of the island. They will work their way south until they meet up with the Navy personnel and dogs."

"You're a hero, Diego." Jessica said. "You saved those women."

"I don't feel like a hero," Diego said, "I wasn't too happy when the captain pointed a gun at me."

"A gun?" She yelled.

"Shhh," He cautioned, "any louder and Cristina will hear clear back to our casa."

"Ooooh, so you haven't told her what's going on?" Jessica said, with mischief in her voice.

"I told her I was delayed with a little problem and would be awhile." Diego sighed, "She was going to wait up for me," He waggled his eyebrows.

"But a gun, crap, that's scary." Jessica said. "Cristina is going to be royally pissed-off at you," she said using her favourite Canadian expression for steaming-hot angry.

"Two guns. The deckhand dropped his pistol and one of the teenagers picked it up. She was waving it around trying to decide who to shoot first; the captain, the kid, or me. Luckily she didn't know how to fire it." Diego said.

"Double crap!"

"I don't think I will mention the weapons when I tell Cristina the story." He added.

Maricruz snorted a laugh. She had been quietly listening as they walked towards the traffickers' boat.

Shaking her head, Jessica said, "not a good idea. She will find out eventually." Then she turned to Maricruz, "Where do you want Sparky to start?" She asked.

"Inside where the passengers were being held. I kept everyone outside, while we waited for the dogs. Both handlers say they won't be back for at least another hour." She said. "We need to find those women."

Jessica lifted Sparky over the gunwales, and placed him on the deck. She unclipped his leash, leaving him to roam and sniff anything that interested him. Keeping one eye on her dog, she asked Maricruz, "According to Diego's description they sound like teenagers, not women. What happens if we do find them?"

A sad look drifted through Maricruz' eyes. "They'll be returned to Cuba, with the other girls that we have in protective custody."

"That sucks," Jessica muttered.

"Yes, it does." Agreed Maricruz, "It truly does."

116

"You know, Maricruz, he's not really trained for this." She said, as she reattached Sparky's lead, then lifted him from the boat to the dock.

"Yes, I know Jess, but I'm desperate."

"What the heck is that awful smell?" Jessica asked, as she sniffed the air around her dog."

"Vomit. The girls had a rough crossing." Maricruz replied.

"Whew, the stench should make it easier for him to find them." Jessica said, wrinkling her nose as she noticed the mess on her dog's paws. "Sparky can you find the girls?"

Sparky glanced up momentarily when she said his name, then continued to nose the area near the hull. He crossed the wharf back and forth a few times, some-what aimlessly.

"He might have something," Diego said, "that's where the two older ones were scuffling with the deckhand."

Jessica's breath caught in her throat, part of her hoped he wouldn't find the girls. There weren't many options in Cuba for young women from poor families. But on the other hand, being held as sex-slaves in some god-forsaken-brothel was worse, far worse.

"What do you think, Jess? Has he got the scent?" Asked Maricruz, as Sparky intently sniffed the dock. He was moving incrementally towards the exit.

"I'm not sure." She responded. Taking care not to crowd her dog, or to hold him back, she ambled behind him.

"At this speed, it will be sunrise before we get to the gates," Diego said with a laugh.

"Oh, I know, Jessica replied. "He's excruciatingly slow when we go for walks. The only things that get exercised are his sniffer, his back right leg, and his bladder."

As she spoke, his tail wagged rapidly a few times, and he moved a little quicker towards the gates. "Try to keep up everyone, we're really moving now!" She quipped.

Chapter 16

February 8th Isla Mujeres

"Shhh," an older girl whispered to the group of teenagers huddled in a dark building. "We must be very quiet."

"But, Carmen, they have a *perro*, it will attack us!" Esme said. Only thirteen-years old she had been strong and determined to escape, until the dog arrived. Originally from the same tiny village in Cuba, Carmen knew Esme had been seriously mauled as a toddler and was still terrified of dogs.

"It's only a small dog, Esme. They are just trying to find us." Carmen put her finger to her lips, "Por favor, be quiet." She had convinced only six of the twenty teenagers to escape with her. The other were terrified of the captain and couldn't be persuaded to run.

"But, I don't want to go to jail." Fifteen-year-old Catalina, loudly wailed.

Carmen sighed, it was hopeless. The dog had stopped searching. He had lifted his head and was looking right at their hiding place. He had either heard Catalina crying or he could smell them. The dog walked towards them, pulling a blonde-haired *gringa* with him. *Please God, don't send us back to Cuba,* Carmen whispered.

~

"Maricruz, did anyone check in there?"

Walking faster to keep up with Sparky, Jessica pointed at a derelict building a block north from the marina gates. She was strong, but when her pooch set his mind to it he could tow her to his chosen destination. Even though he only weighed eleven kilos, about twenty-four pounds, the dog was muscular. Recently Jessica had attached his leash to a friend's wheelchair. Sparky had towed the large man and the wheelchair quite a distance before she stopped laughing and unhooked him. Now, she was hopeful that Sparky was pulling her towards the runaways, but at the same time she was miserable thinking about their bleak future.

"I'm not sure." Maricruz keyed the microphone on her radio and asked the search coordinator if the building had been checked.

He responded, *negative Teniente Zapata*.

"Let me go first, Jess." Maricruz said, striding faster her right hand instinctively touched her holster, checking for her sidearm.

"They are just kids, Maricruz."

"Si, desperate kids." She held up a hand. "Wait here."

Diego ignored Maricruz, and followed a few steps behind. She turned and glared at him. "Diego, I meant you too. These girls have had enough trauma involving men."

He stopped. "You're right, I didn't think of that."

Jessica shortened Sparky's lead by wrapping it around her hand a few times. When she kept him close to her body, she could control his strength better. He was pulling, hard, wanting to investigate the building.

"Sit Sparky. We have to wait." She said, pointing at a spot by her feet. He rebelliously flicked a glance at her command. His butt briefly grazed the ground, then he stood and strained forward. "Sparky! Sit!"

"Do you want me to hold him, Jess?" Diego said, extending his hand to take the leash. "Maricruz might need a hand and men aren't welcome, even the four-legged kind." He shrugged, "it's pretty common for local *ninõs* to be afraid of dogs. Leave him with me."

"Sure, thanks." She unwound the leash and passed it to Diego.

"Crap, he's strong." Diego said, as Sparky tried pull him towards the building.

"Yes, he is. Keep him close, it's easier." Jessica reached down and gently held Sparky's muzzle, until he looked her in the eyes. "You be a good boy." She huffed a laugh at his brief look of defiance. "Brat!" She muttered, walking away.

Jessica could hear several young voices coming from inside the building, some crying, some whimpering and one resolutely arguing with Maricruz.

She heard the lieutenant say in Spanish, "Carmen, please calm down and listen to me." Jessica couldn't understand rapid angry response, but the speaker was definitely not calm.

Dawn was still an hour or more away, but Jessica didn't want to frighten the girls by turning on her bright Maglite. She carefully entered the structure, testing the ground with each step, and reached up feeling for overhead obstructions that could give her head a hard thump. The street light only illuminated the entrance it didn't penetrate into the depths of the building. She shivered, imagining spiders, scorpions, and other fun stuff just waiting to land on her neck.

"Hola chicas," she said softly.

"Jess, I asked you to wait outside." Maricruz said.

"Let me help. They're afraid of your uniform."

Maricruz huffed, but she didn't insist that Jessica leave.

Her eyes were adjusting to the dark interior, and she could just make out the features of a youngster sitting nearby. "Hola, what's your name?" She asked in her awful Spanglish.

"Yoli." Came a faint reply, followed by a loud sniff.

"Yoli, that's a beautiful name. Mine is Jessica." She said, saying Yessica, the way it would be pronounced in Spanish. "Would you like to come outside and meet my perrito?"

"No," Yoli wailed. "Perros bite!"

"No, not my perro." Jessica said, keeping her voice light and friendly. "He's a hero. He helps people."

Yoli sniffed loudly but didn't answer.

Jessica searched in her pocket for her ever-present piece of paper towel, her favourite problem solver. It was useful for wiping her sweaty face, or picking up dog poop, or in this case drying a young girl's tears. She had stuck a fresh piece in her pocket as she left her casa. *No poop.* She held it out, "Here, Yoli, take this."

A hand reached out, "Gracias," she meekly answered, and noisily blew her nose.

Jessica glanced at Maricruz. The lieutenant had a smile on her lips. She gave Jessica a discrete thumbs-up.

The older girl had for the moment stopped arguing and was intently watching Jessica. She could be the one Maricruz had called Carmen.

"I have an idea," Jessica said, thinking of her mother's tactics to deal with her strong-willed brood. "Why don't we have some ice cream, and talk?"

Maricruz stared at her. *What?* She mouthed.

Jessica shrugged, *why not?*

"Ice cream is for babies," Carmen retorted. "We aren't babies, we came here to work."

Oh, yeah, you were definitely going to be working, Jessica thought, but instead answered.

"Ice cream is good for anyone. Come on, you don't want to stay here with the spiders and stuff."

And then the shrieking started.

Jessica clamped her hands over her ears. She had once asked Diego if Shrieking-101 was a mandatory course in the Mexican schools. It was common for adolescents of all ages to shriek, for whatever reason, at high volume and with an ear-splitting pitch. Diego had laughed at her question. He had never noticed. It just part of his culture.

Still screaming the group rushed outside, brushing imaginary spiders from their hair and clothes. Even Carmen moved smartly in the direction of the street. She wasn't panicking, just walking quickly.

"Nicely done, Jessica." Maricruz said with a grin. An odor of vomit, sweat, and fear drifted in the air as she followed the teenagers. She keyed her handset, "We're coming out. Keep the girls together."

Chapter 17

February 8th Sunrise

Fuentes thumbed the screen on his phone, checking for messages or missed calls. Nothing. He scrubbed a hand over his face, willing himself to stay awake. *Where the hell was Sánchez?* The captain and his nephew were not answering the radio, or their cellphones.

Did he make it to Isla Mujeres? Or was he still trying to limp his boat to Cancun? Fuentes was confident that Sánchez had enough sense to hide somewhere before dawn. He wouldn't want a helpful local offering to tow them to a marina. There was no believable explanation for a group of young women drifting in a disabled vessel with two men. Two armed men.

Their boss, Rafael Fernandez, was an early riser. He would be calling Fuentes for an update any minute now. If he knew their location he could send out a second boat to collect the women, and leave the captain and the deckhand to sort out their mechanical problems. But Alejandro was either dealing with another problem, or avoiding him.

What a monumental screw-up!

Fuentes gripped his chin, thinking. He nodded once and keyed another number.

"Si, Bueno." Came the sleepy reply.

"Wake up your crew. I want the families of Alejandro Sánchez and his nephew picked up, *pronto*. The kid's name is Ruben Pech. He lives near Sánchez."

"I know the houses," The other man paused, "are you sure about this?"

"Do it!" Fuentes coldly replied, and disconnected. He'd try once more on the radio to contact Sánchez, then it was just too damn bad what was going to happen next. Striding to the control room, he keyed the radio transmitter.

"Musician. This is Casa Grande." He said. Silence.

"Musician, this is Casa Grande." He repeated, then added, "We have invited your families to the fiesta. Contact us ASAP." That should pucker the man's sphincter.

~

"Shhh!" Diego said, holding up his hand in a stop motion. He thought he had heard a voice coming from the traffickers' boat.

"Musician, this is Casa Grande." A male voice said, "We have invited your families to the fiesta. Contact us ASAP."

Diego glanced at his yawning brother-in-law. Pedro nodded his head. He had heard it too.

They waited in silence. Five minutes, ten minutes. Nothing.

"What do you suppose that was about?" Diego asked.

"It could be nothing, but who organizes a fiesta at this time of the morning?" Pedro replied. He yawned again and stretched. "I need a monster-sized jolt of caffeine."

"What's the matter? You couldn't keep up with your girlfriend and her buddies?" Diego teased referring to the beautiful and tough *Teniente* Maricruz Zapata.

"Hell no," Pedro laughed, "I called it quits after two hours of crashing through the bug-infested bushes."

Diego grinned at Pedro's admission of not being as fit as Maricruz, but he was still puzzled by that radio message. "I'm going to have a quick look around." He said stepping aboard. "God, the stench!" He covered his mouth and nose with one large hand.

"I know, the galley is awash in vomit." Pedro said.

Diego backed away from the door to the galley. The radio transmission was picking at his brain, telling him something. Usually radio calls were addressed to the name of the boat. This vessel was the *Maria Elena*. Maybe he had heard it wrong?

"Pedro, what names did you hear in that transmission?"

"Casa Grande was calling the Musician."

"You're sure? Not the *Maria Elena*?"

"No, Musician."

"That's what I heard too." Diego turned to step off, when a white triangular-shape caught his eye. It was stuck in a corner of the dashboard. He picked at it, until he could grasp a piece and pull it free. A business card for a Cancun group of mariachis! Musician!

~

"Empty!" Fuentes roared. "What the hell do you mean, empty?"

"Exactly what I said, both houses were empty. No people."

"They could be out somewhere, taking their kids to school, or at work." Fuentes said, glaring at the young punk whose nick-name was Chewy.

"No, it looks like they grabbed whatever they could and ran." Chewy replied, "The doors weren't even locked."

Fuentes scowled at the juvenile thug. He could see Chewy wanted to sneer at him, but was for the moment he was still cowed by Fuentes position in the organization. *How much longer,* he wondered, *before the Don's anger turned against him?*

"Get your lazy ass back out there and ask around." He ordered. "Someone must know where they are."

Chewy glowered at him, then turned and strode away.

As Fuentes reluctantly hovered his finger over Fernandez's number the phone rang. Unknown number, flashed on the screen. "Si, Bueno."

"This is your friend." A voice said.

Fuentes didn't answer. He had dozens of snitches providing information.

"The friend that works on an island." The voice said.

Ah, the rookie police constable on Isla. "Que pasa?" What's up? He asked.

"Your packages are being held."

"Where?"

"At the bigger storage unit near the boats," The man answered, meaning the naval base in Centro, and not the police station located in the colonias.

"Claro," Fuentes said, saying he understood the man's hint. "What happened to the deliverymen?"

"The vehicle was abandoned." The cop replied. "We're looking for them. They might be sick or injured."

"Claro. I will complain to their head office about the delivery delay." Fuentes said, playing along with the courier theme. "Keep me updated." He said and disconnected without waiting for a response.

From bad to worse. The women were in custody at the Navy base. The captain and the deckhand were missing. The boat was confiscated. The two families who would have been an alternate target for the *Don's* rage had disappeared, obviously warned by Sánchez. And, he was still under orders to kill the people who had unintentionally hampered the *Don's* drug distribution system on Isla a few months ago.

Just freaking wonderful.

Chapter 18

February 8th Isla Mujeres

"Si, Bueno." Carlos said as he answered his cellphone.

"Mornin' Carlos, I have a big favour to ask," Jessica said.

"Hola chica," He glanced at Yasmin, mouthing *Jessica*. He set her second cup of coffee in front of her, prepared just the way she liked it strong, mixed with hot foamy milk and drizzled with caramel syrup. "What do you need?"

Yasmin winked and blew him a kiss.

Jessica said, "I've been up all night. I'm hoping that you can find someone else to take my shift today."

"Are you sick?" Carlos asked. Jessica was a reliable worker. She never missed a shift. He picked up his second cup of coffee and took a cautious sip, testing the temperature before gulping a mouthful.

"No, but it's complicated." She replied, "Maricruz called me around two-thirty this morning. She wanted Sparky to track a group of girls."

"What?"

"As I said, it's complicated," She rapidly carried on with her explanation, "A boatload of young Cubans ended up on the island. The Navy and the police are still searching for the two men that brought them here. Some of the girls escaped and Maricruz needed another dog to track them."

"Another dog?" He asked, sitting down at the table. He nodded and gestured, *momentito,* as Yasmin peppered him with whispered questions. He could feel her impatient curiosity, wanting to know what was happening.

"Yes, the two dogs were already tracking the men, who had split up and went in different directions." Jessica said, "Sparky found the girls. I convinced them to come with us." She added, with a slight laugh in her voice.

"I hear another story in that laugh."

"I'll tell you later." She said. "So, you are okay about me not working tonight?"

"No problem, I'll call Inez. She's asked for extra shifts, because her son needs dental work."

"Okay great. I'm going to get some sleep. Chat later."

"Sleep well." Carlos said, and disconnected the call.

"Tell me," Yasmin reached across and lightly grasped Carlos' arm, "what's going on?"

"It's another Jessica and Sparky adventure." Then he repeated what Jessica had said.

"Ever since she adopted Sparky" Yasmin huffed, "she just can't stay out of trouble."

Carlos pinned his chocolate-brown eyes on Yasmin's annoyed face. He cocked one eyebrow, "The way I remember it, you and Jessica were already knee-deep in trouble when she found him." He was referring to their illegal treasure-hunting incident. That adventure could have landed both women in jail, or Yasmin jailed and Jessica deported from Mexico.

"Well," Yasmin squirmed, "our big day is just two weeks away. I don't want the maid-of-honour to be a scratched up mess."

"God help anyone who messes up The Wedding," he said, sarcastically gesturing air quotes with his fingers.

Yasmin tilted her head and gave him *the look*. The one that said, *don't push this too far*.

He loved the feisty, adventurous Yasmin, much more than the neurotic-event-planner version that had been so prevalent in these last few months. It was good to see a flash of her strong personality.

He stood up, and planted an intense kiss on her lips. "Damn, I love you woman!"

~

Maricruz shed her gear, dumping everything on an empty chair. Hot, itchy and bug-bitten under the heavy equipment and the camo gear she needed a shower, food, and six hours of uninterrupted sleep. Instead her commanding officer had ordered her written report to be on his desk in one hour.

She unscrewed the cap on a bottle of water, tipping it back and emptying the contents before pausing for a breath. She plunked her body into another chair sticking her feet under the desk, and pulled out a stack of blank reports.

She and Jessica had spent two hours cajoling information out of the girls, finding out their full names, the villages they were from, and how they had ended up on a boat headed to Mexico. Carmen had remembered the name of the recruiter, Omar

López Encalada, because he was from a village near her home. Carmen described him as handsome and always kind to her family. She remembered him telling her parents that he had a good job waiting for her in America. He had promised his cousin and his wife would watch over her.

"How old are you?" Maricruz had asked.

"I am sixteen." Carmen had proudly said, "I want to work and send money home to my family."

Maricruz had wanted to wrap the girl in her arms and weep. Instead she nodded reassuringly and continued probing for details. Perhaps if she had enough information the authorities could track the leader of the trafficking ring.

She huffed out a breath. It wouldn't be the Navy officers arresting the men, it would be the policía and money talked. The criminals would buy their way to freedom.

In the meantime the girls would be kept under guard on the base. They wouldn't be allowed to leave, but they would be safe, clean and fed. At some point the commander would be forced to turn them over to the immigration authorities, and they would be deported back to angry, disappointed parents. She hoped the parents hadn't intentionally given their children to the traffickers. If they had been accomplices in the arrangement then their daughters would not be welcomed home. They would be seen as a failed opportunity, a financial burden.

Maricruz fiddled with her device. The screen displayed the time and date; only two more weeks until Carlos and Yasmin's big day. In fourteen days she would be wearing gorgeous deep purple floor-length gown and matching high heels, with her hair piled in a seductive up-do. Yasmin had hired a make-up artist and hairdresser who would spend the morning beautifying the women. It would be a social, chatty, hectic morning followed by a night of laughter, decadently rich food, too much wine, and dancing. She loved to *salsa*. That dance suggested love-making with every step, every hip wiggle, and every twirl. She smiled at the thought of dancing with Pedro. He was stocky and muscular, but oh, that man had moves.

Maricruz reluctantly picked up a pen. She knew the printer was out of ink, again. She would have to handwrite her report. She fingered the edges of the blank reports thinking of the unfairness of life. She worked hard, but she had a happy safe life. The young Cuban women faced a bleak future. As Jessica would say, *it sucked.*

Chapter 19

February 8th Isla Mujeres

Trying to appear relaxed and bored Alejandro Sánchez leaned against a concrete wall at the crowded passenger ferry terminal. His boarding ticket poked out of a breast pocket. He was prepared to slip around the corner into the busy taxi ranks if he thought he was being closely scrutinized. Alejandro anxiously scanned the crowd, searching for his nephew Ruben Pech.

They had separated during the night in an attempt to confuse the search dogs. Wading knee-deep in the ocean and plowing through the spooky, tangled mangroves he had managed to shake the two men and the dog that had been tracking him. His pulse vibrated with fear at the possibility of running into a hungry crocodile or a boa constrictor. Every splash of water, every snake-shaped mangrove root that he tripped over spiked his breathing. He was exhausted. And worried.

His nephew had never been in trouble with the policía. If arrested he would be terrified and easy to flip, blabbing what little he knew about the *Don's* system. Penalties for human trafficking were harsh with the possibility of a jail sentence of thirty or more years. Alejandro also knew that if Ruben was captured, Fernandez would have the kid killed inside the jail.

Before they separated Sánchez had taken the pistol from Ruben and tossed both of their guns into the sea. In Mexico possession of a firearm or even a single round of ammunition carried a penalty of five years in prison. They had enough problems without adding possession of firearms to the list. But more than that, Sánchez had noticed the previously un-armed municipal police who patrolled the island were now carrying side-arms. An inexperienced and newly-armed cop plus a scared teenager with a gun would lead to disaster. Their only hope was to escape the island without being apprehended.

Movement caught his attention and he shifted his gaze. The jet-propelled blue and yellow Ultramar ferry was nosing into the dock, about to unload the passengers. In a few minutes he could board, taking him one step closer to safety.

Alejandro glanced at his iPhone. He couldn't decide whether to keep it or destroy it. He had taken the battery out to reduce the chances that he could be tracked but he was still uneasy. Not knowing what her dear *papi* did for a living, his teenage daughter Sofia had casually shown him all the free programs she called apps available to track cell phones. She had scared him half-to-death with her nonchalant knowledge of electronic monitoring. Until then he had no idea how easy it was to find a person even when the person didn't want to be found.

He studied the treacherous device in his hand. He desperately wanted to call his wife and make sure she and his sister had followed his earlier instructions. He needed to know they were safe but he was afraid to activate his phone. Maybe once he was on the Cancun side of the bay he would try a quick call to his wife just to be sure she was okay. Then he remembered, he had explained what Sofia had taught him; anyone can be tracked via their cell. He had told her to remove the battery from her iPhone. He would have to wait until he could safely visit their hiding place. He hoped she didn't panic and try to call him.

A group of men and women began to stream off the docked passenger ferry. Most of the commuters were wearing logoed shirts of whatever company they worked for; hotels, restaurants, grocery stores, and dive shops. The line-up inside the terminal started moving as shoppers and a mix of construction workers and day labourers headed into Cancun.

He casually placed himself at the back of the line. His chin was pointed down as his eyes nervously scanned his surroundings. Ahead of him two local men gossiped noisily about the policía pursuit of two heavily-armed men, rumoured to be dangerous drug-runners. Sánchez had to stop himself from snorting a laugh. Dangerous men; a worried forty-year-old dad and a frightened teenager.

He handed his ticket to the attendant, who tore off a section and returned the stub to him, "Gracias," Sánchez mumbled.

"*De nada, tenga buen diá.*" Replied the attendant already looking towards the next person in line.

Sánchez walked up the ramp, nodding at the deck hand as he stepped inside the passenger cabin. *So far so good.* He restrained the urge to cross himself. Instead he said a mental prayer asking for assistance, and offering a promise to get out of the trafficking business. He would change his name and move his family someplace remote, a long way away from Cancun and Rafael Fernandez.

Chapter 20

February 8th Isla Mujeres

In four quick steps Ruben strode up the stairs and into the ferry terminal. The docks were located just off a double-wide street divided by a boulevard of palms trees. As he entered the waiting area he saw a blue and yellow catamaran ferry easing away from the docks, but a posted schedule promised a departure every thirty minutes.

He blew out a breath. He didn't want to hang around in a public place for thirty minutes, but he had to get off the island somehow. He was scared, bug-bitten, dirty, hungry and almost penniless. He studied the crowd around him, most were young males who looked like they were casual labourers headed to the city. It was a common sight to see men of all ages gathered at various corners in Cancun, waiting for someone to stop by and hire them for a day or two. It was a tough hand-to-mouth existence. With his scruffy appearance he would blend in with the others. Just another worker hoping to earn a bit of money.

Temptation Isla

This was Ruben's first time back to Isla in several years. Before his father had abandoned the family, he had taken everyone to the island for a day trip. They had carried a cooler of food and drinks with them, spending the day on the public beach and gleefully playing in the ocean. It was his one good memory of his abusive father.

Today, the island was much busier than he remembered. It was still too early for the tourist-oriented stores and golf cart rental companies to be open, but he had noticed dozens of motos, taxis, and private vehicles. Many seemed to be parents taking their children to school. Every school had a different set of colours for the uniforms that all school-aged kids had to wear. As a teenager he had hated his school uniform, until he realized the standard-issue clothing was financially easier on his single mom. There was no money for trendy clothes. They were lucky that his uncle Alejandro had helped keep a roof over their heads and food in their stomachs. When money was tight the family meal consisted of a few tortillas with hot sauce and a shared bottle of Coke, but it filled the hole in his stomach.

He hopefully scanned the waiting area, looking for his uncle. *No luck.* He noticed the sign for *baños*, and headed that way. *Might as well take a leak, and search Alejandro at the same time.* Five minutes later he exited the washrooms. No Alejandro.

Ruben scanned the crowd again looking for his uncle then headed to the ticket counter on the other side of the waiting area.

"That's a ridiculous amount of money for a fifteen-minute ride." he said. "I heard you ask that man for a much lower amount," He pointed at a person walking away from the ticket counter.

The ticket agent replied. "Only residents with the approved identification or a senior with an INAPAM card qualify for the reduced rates."

"I don't have that much money and I have to get to Cancun. My dad had a serious heart attack, he's in the hospital. I have to get there immediately." Ruben said, trying to soften her resolve. He didn't have enough money for the fare.

The agent shook her head, "I am really sorry, but I can't help you. Take the car ferry. It's slower but inexpensive for foot passengers."

Ruben suddenly realized he was drawing unwanted attention to himself. The people waiting in line behind him were becoming restless, wanting to purchase their tickets. "I'm new to the island." He said, "Where is the car ferry?"

She pointed with her right arm, "About three blocks south. You can't miss it."

145

"Gracias."

"De nada," She said then glanced over his shoulder at the next person in line, already dismissing him.

"Hola Luis. How are you today?" Ruben heard the woman say as he stepped away from the counter. He caught a glimpse of a slim well-dressed man smiling at the ticket agent.

Ruben knew he would have to pass the Navy base to get to the car ferry, but he had no other choice. His gut clenched with anxiety. He hoped the dogs and their handlers had returned to quarters and weren't still searching for him.

He had no idea when the next car ferry departed, but at the moment it was his only option. Ruben walked in the direction the woman had pointed, keeping his head down. Everything had happened so quickly last night. The older girl Carmen had led an outbreak of girls and two of them had shoved him into the water. His gun had fallen on the dock, and another girl had snatched it up, shakily pointing it at his uncle. Then a man appeared out of the thick foliage near the exit gates and told them the police and the *Marinas* were on the way.

His uncle had aimed his gun at the man telling him to stay out of his business, but they had heard the sirens and seen the flashing emergency lights. It was time to run and hope for the best.

He had thrown his phone in a garbage can as he ran from the tracking dog. He hadn't thought to remove the battery, but he was pretty sure the device was useless after the dunking in the ocean.

He walked up to the booth in the parking lot, "When is the next sailing?" He asked.

"It leaves in fifteen minutes." The woman replied.

"Okay, I would like a foot-passenger ticket please." Ruben said, noting that the price was about a quarter of what the faster ferry cost.

"Your ticket is only valid for the next sailing." She said, and pushed the slip of paper and his change towards him.

"How long does the crossing take?"

"About forty-five minutes." She replied, and pointed at a low structure off to one side of the parking lot. "There is a small waiting room over there."

"Gracias," He said, and headed towards the building. He counted his change. He had just enough to buy a bottle of water from the snack counter.

As he settled on a narrow bench with a view of the ferry ramp, two black pickup trucks overflowing with police officers arrived at the terminal. Ruben's heart felt as if it had stopped beating. *What the hell? How did they find me here?*

Immobilized by fear he stared at the group of men and women. There were about a dozen standing inside the truck's box, while a few balanced on the back bumper. His panicked gaze examined their hands. *Were they reaching for guns?* No their holsters were empty.

Individually, the officers scribbled on a piece of paper attached to a clip board. They appeared to be signing for the ferry fare. Some plopped tiredly onto the concrete seawall, others removed their dark blue uniform shirts exposing plain t-shirts underneath.

A loud noise jolted his attention away from the policía. The ferry had arrived. The ramp lowered with a loud bang. Foot passengers streamed off, including another large group of police constables. The two groups mingled, greeting each other with hand slaps, fist bumps or hugs. The new arrivals climbed into the two waiting pickups that departed in a rush.

Shift change. Ruben gratefully relaxed his breathing. A friend had once told him that the island cops worked twenty-four hour shifts. One day on. One day off. Sleep and eat, and then back to work for another twenty-four hours.

While he had been panicking over the arrival of the policía the deckhands had organized the departure of the onboard vehicles. As soon as the traffic cleared the ship, the policía and other foot passengers walked aboard. It appeared to be the normal routine. Ruben slowly stood up, and began to tread towards the ferry. With each step he felt as if he was walking towards his execution.

As the crowd neared the two stairways they formed a single file and tramped up the rusty metal treads to the upper deck. Ruben watched with relief as the policía scattered along the narrow benches and flopped into horizontal positions. Many were asleep before the ferry left the dock.

The cops were exhausted and not the least bit interested in any of the passengers, including him.

He stuffed himself into a narrow corner and pretended to doze.

Chapter 21

February 8th Isla Mujeres

Diego repeatedly flicked the edge of the business card with his thumbnail as he puzzled over the recent events.

First there was that odd radio transmission: *Musician, this is Casa Grande. We have invited your families to the fiesta. Contact us ASAP.*

Then when he searched the traffickers' boat he had found the printed card with the name of a mariachi band and a contact number, but no other information. The background photo was a group of men in traditional mariachi costumes wearing large sombreros. Their faces were indistinct.

Diego was only guessing, but he thought *Musician* could be the code name for the boat captain. The rest of the message didn't make a lot of sense ... unless it was a threat. *We have your families. Call us.*

Who should he pass this information to? Teniente Maricruz of the Marinas, or Sergeant Ramirez of the municipal policía?

Cristina set a large mug of hot coffee on the table in front of him with one hand, and reached to still his obsessive flicking with her other hand. "Diego, please stop," She said. "You're driving me crazy."

"I'm sorry, carina. I was thinking."

"I know, but you are so tired, you're a zombie." She teased. "Drink the coffee, or go to bed."

"I'll drink the coffee. I have a couple of calls to make."

"Would you like some breakfast then? Maybe *huevos rancheros*?"

"Perfect, I'm famished." Thinking of the delicious combination of corn tortillas stuffed with cooked eggs then smothered with a chili, tomato, and onion salsa, Diego's mouth filled with saliva. "Could I have four?" He asked.

Cristina laughed, "You can eat more than that."

Diego smiled, his wife knew him too well, "Tina, I'm sorry I wasn't here to help you get our ninõs to school."

"I managed. You were busy helping those poor girls," She said, piling his breakfast onto a plate. Cristina kissed him, and set the plate down. "You are my hero."

"Does your hero rate a second cup of coffee?" He asked holding up his mug, a cheesy smile on his face.

She laughed, "I could use Jessica's favourite response – do you have a piano tied to your ass? But, today you are my super-hero. At midnight you will revert to being a mere mortal."

Diego grinned, then picked up the first egged-stuffed tortilla crammed half of it in his mouth. He chewed rapidly, swallowed quickly, ate the remainder and snatched up the next one. Between bites he slurped gulps of coffee. Using the last bite of tortilla he wiped the remaining tiny morsels from of his plate, popped it in his mouth and swallowed. He leaned back and patted his bulging stomach. *Muy rico, gracias, mi amor.*"

"I'm surprised you could taste anything." Cristina gave him a bemused look as she removed his plate, "You ate like a starving dog."

~

"Bueno," A female voice answered.

"Alexis?" Diego asked confirming that he was speaking to Alexis Gomez. She was the police constable who worked and lived with Sergeant Felipe Ramirez.

"Si,"

"It's Diego. I'm looking for Felipe. Is he home?"

"Si, but," She snickered, "He's ... busy at the moment."

Diego heard Felipe's deep voice in the background, "She means I'm taking a dump." Then he heard a toilet flushing and water running.

"I hope you washed your hands," Diego kidded when Ramirez finally answered the phone.

"Never," Ramirez retorted. "What's up?"

"Do you know about last night's incident at the marina?"

"Traffickers, twenty young women, the men escaped, boat in custody." Ramirez rapidly summarized, "Our crew was dispatched to search the boats in Centro."

"I might have stumbled on a clue to the captain's identity." Diego said, then gave Felipe a quick recap of the radio message and his discovery of the business card. "Do you want it, or should I take it to the station?"

"Give me a minute." Ramirez said, "I need something to write on. Okay, give me the number."

Carlos recited the ten digits.

"Gracias, I'll get the card from you after we sleep for a bit."

"Claro, I think I'll do the same."

~

Four hours later Ramirez reluctantly pulled the sheet back and swung his feet onto the floor. His damn brain wouldn't stop spinning. He carefully eased out of bed, trying not to wake Alexis.

"Qué hora es?" A muffled voice, asked what time is it.

"Too early to get up. Go back to sleep."

"Okay."

He grinned as she turned on her stomach and buried her head under her king-sized pillow. It was her way of shutting out the lights and sounds of their lively neighbourhood. Hopefully she'd stay that way for at least four more hours.

Today was their day off, tomorrow they would work another twenty-four-hour shift, and then get the following day off. Eat, work, sleep, and repeat. Occasionally they remembered to include a night out with friends, and a little *chucka-chucka*, a bit of fun between the sheets.

He was still bone-tired, but intrigued by the information Diego had passed along. Padding barefoot to the bathroom he relieved himself, remembering to lower the toilet seat for Alexis. From past experience he knew if she happened to woozily stumble out of bed, and fall ass-first into the toilet she would holler a colourful collection of profanities at him. Living in a thickly-populated *colonia* had its disadvantages. Their neighbour Marcel thought it was funnier than hell when he heard Alexis cussing at Felipe.

He pulled on his favourite O'Neill shorts, closed the bedroom door behind himself and moved into their tiny living-eating space. He unplugged his phone from the charger, and quietly opened their front door. It was best to talk outside. Mamma-bear needed her sleep or she would turn into Cranky-bear.

"Detective Toledo," He said when the call was answered. "This is Sergeant Ramirez from Isla Mujeres." He hadn't spoken to the man for a few months, so he asked, "Do you remember me?"

"Si, of course. What's up?" The detective from the Cancun office of the State Policía replied.

Felipe lowered the volume on his voice. "Got a few minutes?"

"Si, momentito." He could hear the slap of Toledo's footsteps as he walked across a tile floor. "Okay, go ahead."

"Do you know about our recent incident with the traffickers?"

"Indirectly," He said, "Not my assignment. No homicide. So, no homicide detectives needed." Toledo replied. "Fill me in."

His eyes continuously scanning his surroundings, Ramirez spent the next fifteen minutes quietly relating his information and answering Toledo's questions.

"Huh!" Toledo said, "Just a wild-ass guess, but I would put money on Rafael Fernandez being the importer."

"That was my first thought. But, who's the Musician?"

"No clue. I'll call the number. I need a mariachi band to impress my wife on our upcoming anniversary." Toledo said.

"You ... are married?" Ramirez joked. He remembered Toledo as a hard-faced Latino, a younger version of Tommy Lee Jones in the 1990's spoof *Men in Black*. He even dressed like the movie character Agent K, black suit, white shirt and skinny black tie.

"Of course," Toledo retorted. "I'm an amazing catch!"

Ramirez was still chuckling when they ended the call.

Chapter 22

February 9th Isla Mujeres

"This is the perfect gift for Yasmin." Dante Lopez said, handing Carlos an intricately carved pendant suspended on a delicate gold chain. "It's made from rare blue jade."

"Blue jade? I thought jade was green?" He was standing inside the Mr. Opal jewellery store on Avenida Francisco Madera.

"Jade is an ornamental mineral. If it's composed of calcium and magnesium it is called nephrite. If it's made of silicate of sodium and aluminium it is called jadeite. The colour is most commonly green or white, with sometimes a shot of pink, brown or lavender. But our ancestors valued the blue jade above all the others."

Carlos smiled. Lopez was warming to his two favourite subjects, jewelry and Mayan history.

"It comes from the Motagua River area in Guatemala." He said, "In ancient times only royalty was allowed to wear blue jade."

"Verdad?" Intrigued Carlos asked, "What happened if someone else wore it?"

"They were sacrificed."

"En serio? Are you serious?" Carlos asked.

"Very."

"But if I buy this for Yasmin, wouldn't that be tempting the gods a little?

Lopez grinned, "That was then. This is now. You're not superstitious are you?" He teased.

"No, not really." Carlos laughed self-consciously, "Well, maybe just a little." He admitted. "But this is such a beautiful piece."

"She will look like a Maya queen wearing that necklace."

The stone felt pleasantly warm to the touch as Carlos gently rubbed his fingers over the intricate design. "Okay, you've convinced me. I'll buy it."

Dante gently took the piece from Carlos, polished the stone with a soft cloth and nestled it into its display box. "Would you like me to gift wrap it?"

"You know how to gift wrap?" He said, looking at Dante's wide hands.

"Just because I'm a big man, doesn't mean I'm clumsy. Who do you think carved this beautiful pendant?"

Carlos laughed, "You know Yasmin thinks you are hot when you salsa."

In the tight space of his tiny store the man spontaneously executed a series of graceful salsa moves, "Of course I am!" He laughed, *"Muy caliente!"*

~

"Are you sure this is the right place?" Detective Marco Cervera asked his partner. Standing inside the modest casa, Marco crossed one arm across his chest and propped his chin in the other hand, considering the scene.

The detectives had hollered 'policía' and walked in through the open door, thoroughly searching the home for occupants or victims. All they found were signs of a hurried departure, items scattered as people quickly gathered what was necessary or important to them.

Detective Marco Cervera and Detective Dante Toledo of the State Police, Cancun had been partners for several years. Their fellow officers referred to them as *los gemelas*, the twins, even though their physical appearances were quite different.

Cervera was pushing fifty and thick around the middle. His short dark hair was flecked with grey and he had the rumpled face of a sad Basset hound. Toledo was thirty, skinny, acne-scarred skin and slicked-back hair. He exuded a don't-mess-with-me vibe.

The nickname, the twins, had started because of their preference for black suits, white shirts, skinny black ties and shiny black shoes. But more than once the movie characters from *Men in Black* had been mentioned.

"Si, it's the right house. When I called the number that Ramirez gave me it was answered by the mariachi group's leader. He said this is where Alejandro Sánchez the lead trumpet player lives but he hasn't been able to find him." Toledo answered.

"You identified yourself as policía?" Cervera questioned. Normally locals didn't willingly offer information to the police. They usually had to be firmly persuaded to help.

"Hell no, I said I wanted to book the group for our anniversary party." Toledo said.

Cervera still didn't understand, and shot his partner a questioning look.

"I told him that I had met Sánchez at another event and my wife was a big fan. I said when her father was a young man he played lead trumpet in a Guadalajara mariachi group."

"Did he? Play lead trumpet?"

"He played trumpet in a school band," Toledo replied. "The story worked. I got the information I needed."

Listening to Toledo, Cervera's lips tweaked into an admiring grin. His partner possessed a quick and creative mind. Many times he had heard Toledo invent a believable scenario, like this one, in what seemed like a millisecond.

"Evidently, Sánchez missed an important gig yesterday and the others weren't happy about it. They had to substantially reduce their price for the performance." Toledo shrugged, "I asked him for the address, said I would stop by and ask Sánchez to contact the leader."

"You get a cell number?"

"Si. No answer," Toledo replied. "While you were searching the back, I checked with a neighbour. The sister and her kids have disappeared too."

"So, he's definitely in hiding." Cervera inclined his head, staring at the floor as he considering the information, "Hiding from us and his employer."

"My bet is on Rafael Fernandez." Toledo said, "But as I said to Ramirez, no body, not our case."

"No body — yet." Corrected Cervera.

Chapter 23

February 20th Isla Mujeres

"Jake! Matt!" Jessica yelled. She bounced up and down on her toes waving her arms overhead. "Hey, hey! Over here!" She hollered.

Luis Aguilar reached out a hand and steadied Jessica as she tripped on Sparky's leash. Sparky was excited. Jessica was excited. Luis was apprehensive. He and Jessica had a thing, but neither one of them was sure what that meant. *Committed? Not-committed? And what did her family think about their vague relationship?*

Luis saw a tall, dark-haired man look up and yell. "Jessie!" He had been searching for his luggage in amongst the heap of bags being off-loaded by the deckhands. An even taller, blonde-haired man pointed, waved a long-limbed arm then bent his head. He appeared to be speaking to a shorter person, which in this part of the world was three-quarters of the population.

It was all in your perspective, Luis told himself as he stuck a finger in his ear, the one closest to Jessica's yelling. Mayas were considered to be short by gringo standards, but when compared to someone from say Chiapas, the Mayas considered themselves to be normal-sized. From a distance the two men appeared very similar. Gigantic.

Jessica had assured him they were easy to tell apart. Jake was the oldest, with blue eyes like their mother and white-blonde hair. Matt resembled their dad, he had hazel eyes and reddish-brown hair. Jessica said the combination of reddish hair colour and pale skin was referred to as *a ginger*. Whatever, the two giants were about to meet the on-again, off-again lover of their precious baby sister. Luis guesstimated he was a good head shorter and about two-thirds the size of either one of the brothers.

No problemo, Luis assured himself. *I run marathons. I just have to be a little faster than two angry bulls.*

As the crowd around the baggage thinned Luis asked, "Are those people also family?" He pointed at a tall, older man and two women following the younger men.

"Yes! Mom, Dad, Auntie Pattie!" She hollered again, speeding past the dock attendant's outstretched arm and straight at her family.

Luis caught the eye of Lupe, the ticket-taker who had tried to stop Jessica and the dog from barging into the paid-fare-only zone. "Lo siento. Familia." He said, giving her a what-can-you-do smile and a slight shrug of his shoulders.

"Claro, no problemo." Lupe smiled, as she watched the enthusiastic greeting.

Fascinated, Luis watched her brother Jake intercept Jessica before she reached her parents. She dropped Sparky's lead and leapt into his arms. He pulled her into a bear-hug that lifted her feet off the ground. When he set her down the other brother, Matt, repeated the performance.

Grizzly bears, not bulls. Luis mused. *I can still outrun them.*

Closely following Jessica's every move Sparky vied for attention. Luis could see people bend down to pat him, then carefully step over or past the short, stocky dog dragging his leash. His tail beat the air, like a white flag in a stiff breeze.

The father, although a tall man himself was shorter than his two sons, and appeared happy to squeeze his daughter in a fierce hug with her feet still touching the dock. Then Jessica turned to the two women, who Luis deduced, were her mother Anne Sanderson and her aunt Pattie Packard. She hugged and kissed each one affectionately.

Lupe, the dock attendant, walked over to the group, and politely indicated they should clear the dock. She pointed back at the long line of people walking towards the ferry.

It amused Luis to hear Jessica say, "I'm sorry, I'm sorry," as she quickly scooped up Sparky's leash, then herded her family towards the terminal. She had once explained that repeatedly apologizing for small social blunders was a common Canadian habit.

"Everyone, this is my friend Luis Aguilar." Jessica said, as the group approached him.

"Hi Luis, good to meet you. My name's Gord." The older man said, engulfing Luis's slender hand in his wide palm.

"Mucho gusto, it is a pleasure to meet you Mr. Sanderson." Luis said. Thankfully Gord didn't do that macho hand-crushing-thing that seemed to amuse big men when greeting someone lean and slight like Luis.

"Please, just call me Gord. None of that Mr. Sanderson stuff, it makes me feel old."

"Of course, Gord." Luis replied.

"And, I'm Anne, Jessica's mom." Said one of the women as she stepped closer to give Luis a hug and a buss on the cheek. She then turned and pulled the other woman closer, "And this is my baby sister Pattie."

"Mucho gusto," replied Luis, giving Pattie a light hug as his lips brushed her cheek. Glancing from Anne, to Pattie, to Jessica he was immediately struck by the similarities of the three ladies. Except for their age differences and Jessica's thinner body, they could be triplets. Their features were remarkably alike. Although on second glance he noticed that *Tia* Pattie's hair was a darker colour, closer to the reddish-brown of her nephew Matt. It appeared both sides of the family had a *ginger*.

Jessica's blonde-haired brother stuck out a massive paw and said, "Hi, Luis. I'm Jake." Then cocked a thumb at the other brother, "And this goofball is Matt."

Perplexed, Luis glanced at Jessica. "Goofball?"

"Not a term of endearment."

"Pleased to meet you, Luis," said Matt shaking hands with Luis. "I'm the polite brother. My older brother is a socially inept ape."

"Who're are you calling an ape, little brother?" retorted Jake good naturedly, "You're the one with the orangutan-coloured hair."

"And so it begins," Jessica said rolling her eyes, then she raised her voice to get the group's attention. "I have space for two people, with small suitcases, in my golf cart. The others can get a taxi over there," she said pointing towards the taxi stand. "Just tell the driver that you are staying at Casa Sirena. He'll know the hotel."

"Is that where everyone is staying, Jess?" Asked her mom.

"No, Mom. Casa Sirena is a six-room, funky B&B that I booked mainly for my family. Most of the other guests are booked into the bigger all-inclusive hotels, like the Aluxes, or the Mia." Jessica said, "The Sirena is my favourite hotel on the island. I really hope you like it."

Luis tapped Jessica's arm, "It is close enough you could just drop the first two and come back for the others." He suggested, with a light shrug of his shoulders. "Or, your brothers and I could walk."

She looked at her brothers, "It's only about three or four blocks. Do you want to walk?"

"Sure," Jake answered. "Dad, you hop on Jessica's golf cart. Matt and I can pull yours and Mom's suitcases."

"No," snorted Gord Sanderson. "I'm not an old fart yet. I'll walk and take my own suitcase."

"Gee, how did I know he would say that?" Laughed Anne Sanderson. "Let's get going," she added. "It's getting close to cocktail time, and I'm thirsty."

"Perfect. Casa Sirena has a fun rooftop happy hour just for their guests." Jessica pointed to the right, and said, "My *carito* is over there."

The back and forth banter amused Luis. They sounded like his family, easy-going, teasing but secure in the knowledge that they loved each other — unconditionally. Originally he had been apprehensive when Jessica mentioned she'd invited her family to the island, but the next two weeks could be a lot of fun.

"So, Luis," Jake said, as they towed the suitcases towards the B&B. "How long have you been seeing our sister?"

Here it comes. The big brothers protecting their baby sister.

Chapter 24

February 21st Isla Mujeres

"I'm sure you will find something at the Artist Fair to add to your art collection Auntie Pattie," Jessica said as she drove her golf cart confidently through the narrow streets. Slowing for a large hump in the road, she said, "tope," then shot a quick look at her passenger.

"No worries, I'm hanging on." Pattie said, indicating her right hand wrapped around the plastic safety grip. She also had her right foot extended to block Sparky from getting too close to the edge of the open vehicle. Jessica had assured her that he was happiest by her feet with his ears flapping in the wind.

"Let's see if there is anything you like, and then we will meet everyone for dinner at the *Loco Lobo* at eight o'clock."

"I thought tonight would be the rehearsal. Tomorrow is the big day." Pattie felt a drop or two of rain on her bare legs. "I hope the weather will be nice for the wedding."

"We had the rehearsal and dinner on the 18th," Jessica said, "I think Yasmin is enjoying the long build-up to *the* wedding." She said, then added, "The weather forecast for tomorrow is sunny and warm."

"Good," Pattie said, "But what will you do with Sparky while we are having dinner at the restaurant?"

"He's allowed inside." Jessica said, "He lays under my chair and doesn't fuss, or beg for food."

"Isn't that against the health regulations?"

Jessica waggled her palm in a *mas o menos*, more or less, hand signal, "He's a local hero."

"You're a spoiled little doggie." Pattie said, affectionately rubbing Sparky's head. "I miss my Riley." She added.

"Riley is a wonderful dog, he's so affectionate." Jessica said. "He must be getting on in years by now."

"Yes, he's fourteen now." Pattie said wistfully thinking of her big old Red Setter whom she loved like a son. It had been difficult to leave him at home, but he was too old to endure the frightening experience of travelling as cargo in the belly of the airplane.

Jessica parked in an unlit dirt lot near a small hotel then hopped out of her vehicle.

"Well, damn," Jessica said standing with her fists cocked on her hips, with Sparky's leash gripped in one hand. "There's not many booths set up tonight." She was looking at a meagre row of stalls, with a few strings of white lights draped over a street that was blocked-off by an assortment of orange traffic cones.

Pattie studied the area. She had expected to see a lot of activity, but the area seemed semi-deserted. "This is the artists' fair?" Asked Pattie, she had seen busier neighbourhood rummage sales.

"Yes. It's an outdoor location so when the forecast is for rain, even just a little bit of rain like tonight, a lot of the artists don't show-up." Jessica sighed. A fitful wind blew across the area, causing the vendors to swiftly secure articles that might float away on the breeze.

"A few years ago there were as many as seventy vendors selling everything from original artwork, to interesting photographs, hand-made baskets, bilingual books for children, mystery novels, sea-glass jewellery, homemade food, plus tasty ales from our island brewery." She said.

"What happened?"

Jessica flicked a wry smile at her aunt. "Politics. Lack of municipal support. In-fighting. Complaints from gift store owners." She shrugged.

"We're here. We might as well have a look." Pattie said, walking towards the dozen or so displays. Jessica and Sparky trailed along behind.

One table had a nice assortment of sea-glass jewelry and engraved images. A collection of photographs turned into unique artwork decorated a large section of a crumbling wall, and a grouping of humorous paintings featuring wide-bottomed women was adjacent. Interesting, but the walls of her apartment were already crammed with artwork.

Pattie glanced at Jessica and shook her head, "I don't see anything I need."

"Okay, let's head over to the restaurant. It's almost eight o'clock." Jessica said, checking the time on her phone.

"That sounds good, I'm hungry," Pattie agreed. "But before we go I need to pee, now." She grimaced, "It's an age thing. Where are the public washrooms?"

Jessica craned her neck, looking towards the gloomy Casa de Cultura. "Well, they are over there, but only available sometimes."

"Sometimes?" Pattie asked.

"Yep, sometimes they're open, and sometimes they're not. But I think you are in luck tonight." She pointed towards the building. "I see a light on inside. Go through the entrance, and turn right."

"Okay, back in a jiffy."

"I'll wait here. There are a couple of friends here that I haven't seen recently. Sparky and I can visit with them."

Pattie headed into the women's washroom and opened the door to the first cubicle in the line of four. As soon as she shut the door, the lock and handle fell off – onto the floor outside.

Unconcerned she finished her business, flushed the toilet then stuck her fingers into the hole where the lock had been. Nothing happened. She tried again, with no success.

"Well, damn." Pattie unconsciously mimicked Jessica's expression and stance, as she peered at the bottom of the door.

There was no way that she could squeeze underneath. The gap between door and floor was

175

less than a finger's width. She put her foot on the toilet bowl and stood on the ceramic edge, trying to see over the stall. *Nope!* The metal wall was too high, she couldn't see the other side.

She put one foot on the toilet tank, thinking she could climb over the stall. The tank tottered. It was only attached to the toilet, not the wall.

Give your head a shake woman, you are not thirty years old anymore.

"Jessica! Help!" She yelled. It was stifling hot inside the enclosure, and her shirt was already soaked by perspiration. "Jessica! Help!" She yelled again.

She looked at her cell. It was a new one, purchased to replace her iPhone stolen just before her trip to Mexico. She hadn't transferred her contacts and couldn't remember Jessica's number. *Oh, hell, I'll just call Anne. I know her number.*

"Hello?" Anne Sanderson said. Pattie could hear a background of conversations, and scraping of chairs on tiles floors. It sounded as if group was already at the restaurant.

"Hi sis. I have a bit of a problem." She said, and went on to explain where she was and how she couldn't contact Jessica, who was just outside the building.

"Seriously?" Her sister responded, with a giggle in her voice, "You're stuck in a toilet stall? Hang on a minute."

Pattie could hear her sister's laughter-filled explanation to the group of where she was and why she and Jessica were late for dinner. *Thanks, sis.* She mumbled to herself, *Laugh at my expense.*

"Pattie, Carlos and the boys are on the way to rescue you."

"Tell them to bring me a beer. It's freaking hot in here, and I'm dying of thirst."

"Will do. See you in a few."

~

Occupied by gossipy conversations with island friends, Jessica finally realized that she hadn't seen Auntie Pattie for at least fifteen or maybe even twenty minutes. *It shouldn't take that long to have a pee, even if you are a middle-aged woman.* "Come on Sparky, let's go find her."

"Jessica!" A familiar voice boomed across the street. "Wait," yelled Carlos.

She waved to indicate that she had heard. Striding alongside him were her two stern-faced brothers, Jake and Matt.

What the hell?

Carlos stopped beside her and said, "Did you and the wonder-dog lose someone?" He asked, pointing at Sparky.

"Oh my God. Aunt Pattie. What's happened to her? Sparky and I were just going to look for her in the ladies' room." She blurted out.

"She's locked inside a stall. She has been hollering for you, her favourite niece, to help her," Carlos replied. The men guffawed at her guilty expression.

"You go in first, in case are other women inside." Jake said.

"That's stupid," She retorted. "If anyone has been in the baños recently they would have helped Pattie. Just walk in."

Three male heads shook: No.

"Unbelievable," she snorted, then headed inside. "All clear!" She yelled, then said, "Auntie Pattie are you okay?"

"Hi Jess, I'm fine. Hot, thirsty, my throat is sore from yelling. But I'm okay."

"Hola Pattie," Carlos said, "Just give us a minute and we'll have you out of there." He picked up the handle, reinserted it and tried to open the door. Nothing happened. He took it out fiddled with the mechanism. Still nothing.

"Ah, screw it. Stand back," Jake said. He reached up, grabbed the metal door by the top and yanked it hard. A small piece of steel fell onto the floor, the other part of the broken lock. The door popped open.

Pattie scrambled to escape her airless prison. "Thank you, Jake. I was cooking to death in there!"

Matt reached into his pocket and pulled out a cold cerveza. "But I remembered the beer." He said as he twisted off the cap and handed it to her.

"And you, Matt, are now my very very favourite!" She answered taking a grateful swig.

"Photo op!" Jessie said, pointing at the toilet stall, "Stand inside, and peer around the door with the beer in your hand."

"Perfect." Laughing, Pattie followed Jessica's instructions. "An original piece of Isla art."

Chapter 25

February 22nd Afternoon Isla Mujeres

"Show time!" Jessica whispered to Yasmin. She gently pulled the veil over Yasmin's brimming eyes. "Don't cry sweetie, you will ruin your make-up!" She said, then gave her friend a gentle squeeze before straightening, yet again, the complicated swirl of lace, tiny pearls and satin that pooled around Yasmin's feet.

After all the hours, days, and weeks spent searching for *the perfect dress* Yasmin had finally begged an island seamstress for help. Together they had created what Paloma referred to as a mermaid-dress. Form-fitting from the off-the-shoulder bodice, to mid-thigh it maximized Yasmin's spectacular figure. However, the frothy *tail* of the mermaid was a pain in the butt as far as Jessica was concerned. Once the serious fun started Yasmin would change into a shorter, and equally provocative dress so she and Carlos could *salsa* without her stumbling over a foamy pile of lace and satin.

Jessica winked at Yasmin's teary-eyed papa. Outside the church Oscar Medina had confided to Jessica that he felt sad giving his little girl away to another man, to a new life. She had hugged him and said with a wicked chuckle, "Papa Medina, she's been living with Carlos for months. This is just the formality!"

Oscar had replied with a knowing grin, that a good Mexican papa should always pretend he doesn't know such things about his little girl.

The group of musicians inside the chapel plucked the first cords of *A Thousand Years,* the song that Yasmin had chosen for her entrance. The priest raised his hands, palms up and the buzz of conversation inside the *Capilla de Guadalupe* stopped. The guests stood, turned towards the back of the church ready to catch the action on their cameras and phone apps.

First came Yasmin's nephews, Eduard age seven and Enrique age nine. A freshly-groomed and happy dog walked compliantly between the two young lads. As the little group marched towards the altar their serious demeanor elicited whispered giggles.

The boys had declared they wanted to be

security guards, not assigned the little-kid task of ring-bearers. They were dressed in matching black pants with blue piping and military-style white shirts. In large black letters Ring Security was printed on the back of their shirts. Sparky's black satin vest was printed with Ring Bearer in white letters. Two white satin loops secured the rings to his vest; one on the left shoulder and one on the right.

Jessica cracked open the doors, and took a quick peek. She hoped Sparky was behaving. Diego caught her eye and nodded. All was well. He'd promised to run interference if Sparky stopped to greet friends, or bless a church pew with a little pee.

Next the bridal attendants began their colourful entrance. Maricruz Zapata wore purple, Cristina Avalos lemon-yellow, Carlos's sister Mariana Garcia turquoise, Yasmin's sister Adriana Cetina tangerine, and finally Jessica who had chosen a rich sapphire-blue to compliment her blue eyes.

Flouncing behind Jessica were the flower girls, the three youngest daughters of Luz Hernandez, Carlos' long-time housekeeper and friend. The girls were dressed in mermaid-themed dresses of turquoise, green, and blue. The eldest daughter Anita had argued that real mermaids would scatter sand and sea shells instead of flower petals, until their mother had assured them the priest would be very, very unhappy if that happened.

And then Yasmin and her papa stepped through the door of the church.

~

Carlos was certain his heart had stopped beating as he watched his love, his future, walk towards him. Standing on his left were his childhood friends Diego Avalos, Pedro Velazquez, and Antonio Martinez, plus his two younger brothers Nicolas and Roberto.

"Take a breath man, you are going to pass out," Diego, his best-man whispered as he nudged Carlos with an elbow.

Carlos blinked, and inhaled, then beamed at Yasmin. Through her thin veil he saw her answering smile, and her lips silently formed the words. *Mi amor.*

During the long and complicated church ritual Carlos could only think of the tall slender woman beside him. In unison they knelt, stood, sat, stood again, and then they were repeating their vows to each other.

Her ring fit perfectly, his was a pinch tight but together they managed to push it over his knuckle.

When the priest declared them married Carlos lifted Yasmin's veil and kissed his beautiful wife. The congregation stood and cheered.

It was done!

But first they had to make their way through the mob of family and friends waiting to hug, kiss, and congratulate them.

It was thirsty work! Let the fiesta begin.

~

"Oh, my goodness. This is breathtaking." Exclaimed Anne Sanderson as she gripped her husband's arm. "When Jessica said we would be traveling by boat to the reception, I had no idea this is what she meant."

Gord nodded, "Impressive," he agreed.

A flotilla of colourful pangas bedecked with flowers and ribbons gently bumped against the docks tucked in behind the Bally Hoo Restaurante on Avenida Medina in Centro. The boats were held steady by deckhands as their collection of stylish passengers stepped aboard.

"Look over there, Anne," Pattie said nodding towards the group of guests waiting on the dock. According to Jessica, the men traditionally wore white embroidered linen shirts to formal events, with dark chinos, and trendy well-polished shoes. But Yasmin had added a personal note to the invitations explaining her tropical theme, asking their guests to wear colourful clothing. Most of the men sported the linen shirts in stylish hues that complimented their spouses' outfits; only a few stuck to the conventional choices of white or cream.

Dark-eyed women in perfect makeup, their long dark tresses secured in chic upswept styles picked their way along the dock. Their delicate dresses floated in the light breeze. "These women are stunningly beautiful." Anne remarked. "I feel so dowdy by comparison."

"Yeah, me too." Pattie huffed as she looked down at her simple navy sheath and sparkly sandals.

"You ladies always look fabulous, no matter what you wear," Gord replied. "But did you see the height of those high-heels?" He asked, his eyebrows raised in mock surprise.

"Stilettoes are very fashionable, especially here." Anne replied. "I would love a pair of those shoes."

"What's stopping you, sis?" Pattie asked, ribbing her older sister.

"My knees." Anne replied, thinking how

similar her younger sister and Jessica were, especially when Pattie had that quirky teasing smile on her lips. "I'm on my feet all day at work. High-heels are a thing of the past for me."

"Por favor, Señora," A young man said to Anne. He held out his hand to assist her.

As each panga filled with guests the captains piloted their boats across the bay. "Do you know where are we going?" Gord asked Anne.

"The reception is being held someplace called Zama's Beach Club." She had tucked the invitation into her small handbag. *Just in case.* She wanted to know where they were going and at what time. A warm salty spray dashed against the gunwales, lightly dousing their group. Everyone laughed. It was all part of the adventure.

"Where did Matt and Jake disappear to?" Pattie asked, craning her neck to check for her nephews.

"I caught sight of them helping a group of young ladies board the boats." Answered Gord.

"Helping, right," Anne snickered. "You mean choosing a date for the evening."

Gord slanted a sly grin at her.

"I know what you are thinking, boys will be boys! But those two are in their thirties, and they should be settling down."

"Why? Do you want grandkids?"

"Maybe," Anne said. She hadn't really thought about it, until he asked the question, "someday."

"Like when we are really old?" He teased.

"Okay, yes I want grandkids, but I think I am still too young to actually *be* a grandmother."

Gord was still grinning at her edgy response when their small craft gently nosed against a wharf.

Zama's Beach Club employees dressed in black pants and white shirts rushed to secure the mooring lines and assist the guests onto the dock. As each boat departed another one took its place.

One of the men pointed towards the street and said, "Please walk through the flower-archway, cross the road, and through the main entrance."

As they approached the resort beautiful guitar music and Spanish lyrics beckoned them inside. Pattie stopped and gazed at the amazing decorations; whimsical hearts, candles, gauze-draped walkways, and hundreds of flowers in every imaginable hue. "Wow," She said, her mouth gaping, "just … wow!"

"Close your mouth, sis. Or you'll catch some

flies." Anne teased her sister, but she was right. *Wow ... just wow!*

Chapter 26

February 22nd Late afternoon Isla Mujeres

"Look!" Anne Sanderson pointed at a large white yacht docking in front of Zama's Beach Club. "They came by boat too."

"I bet they didn't get wet," her husband wryly remarked.

Yasmin and Carlos, followed by their bridesmaids, groomsmen, flower girls and ring-security boys disembarked the yacht. One of the restaurant servers stood beside the ramp. His large tray held glasses of champagne for the adults and something fizzy and sweet for the youngsters.

"Let's party!" Shouted Carlos, as he and Yasmin held their champagne flutes aloft to acknowledge the cheers and whistles. "Fiesta!"

Musicians led the boisterous group into the cocktail reception on the upper level at the beach club. Anyone who hadn't been at the church ceremony vied to hug and kiss Yasmin and Carlos.

The servers carefully squeezed between the guests offering beverages and tasty tidbits of food, while a seven-member mariachi band sang romantic Spanish love songs.

Anne smiled as her daughter elegantly glided across the room to give everyone warm hugs. Jessica typically preferred shorts, halter tops and sandals. On the cooler days in Canada she switched to her shabby jeans, warm sweaters and ankle boots. *She cleans up good.* Anne mused.

"Isn't this fabulous?" Jessica said, sweeping an arm to include the festive scene.

"You did tell me that Mexican weddings are amazing," her mom agreed, "but this is incredible."

Jessica laughed. "This is just the warm up to the main event!"

"Sparky was a fabulous ring-bearer." Pattie commented. "So well behaved."

Jessica grinned, "It took a bit of work to convince Yasmin that Sparky would be perfect. She had already asked her two little nephews."

"And I'm sure she wouldn't want to disappoint them." Pattie said.

"Exactly," Jessica agreed. "But the boys wanted to be the security guards instead, so we included Sparky."

"Where is he now? I didn't see him come on the yacht with you."

"No, too many chances for someone to trip with an enthusiastic dog and five excited little kids underfoot." She said, "Luis is bringing him in a few minutes. Sparky can visit with everyone until Carlos and Yasmin have their first dance."

Pattie cocked her head and gave Jessica a questioning look, "Why just until then?"

"The music will get progressively louder as the tequila flows." She said laughing at her aunt's expression. "I think his sensitive hearing would be overwhelmed by noise."

"Mine too!" Pattie said with a smile.

"Has anyone seen Matt and Jake?" Asked Jessica.

Gord smiled and pointed at his sons, surrounded by a group of beautiful young women.

"That didn't take long." Jessica said.

"They don't know much Spanish," Said Pattie eyeing Jake and Matt as they pantomimed and laughed.

"Um ... sex doesn't always need words." Jessica suggestively bounced her eyebrows.

"Excuse me, Jess," The tall, blonde event-coordinator said, "It's time for the bridal party photos on the beach. Tony says the optimum time for lighting is in the next hour."

"Sure, Tiff, no problem." She kissed her mom's cheek. "Chat later." She drifted back towards Yasmin and Carlos who were still surrounded by friends.

"Time for photos!" Jessica circled an arm over her head, "round 'em up and move 'em out!" She said pointing towards the beach.

Diego laughed, "How long have you been waiting to use that corny, old expression?"

"Since I was a kid when we watched old western movies." She bent to sort out the bottom of Yasmin's dress, for the umpteenth time. "How are you doing, Yassy,"

"I'm happy, extremely happy, but everything is a big blur." Yasmin answered, "So many hugs, and kisses, and faces, and names. I'll need photographs to remember everything."

Carlos brushed his lips across hers. "All you have to remember is you are spending the rest of your life with me."

Jessica glanced up, "Hey, no tears. I told you crying will mess up your makeup."

"Too late," She said, as her eyes brimmed

over. "I love you, Carlos Mendoza."

~

"Are we done yet?" Carlos whispered to Yasmin.

"Soon," She whispered back, smiling through yet another series of posed photographs. There had been pictures of the entire group, then bride and groom with each set of parents, then just the bridal attendants and Yasmin, and the groomsmen and Carlos. Comical group compositions that included Sparky. Serious postures. Romantic poses. Now she and Carlos were strolling the dock, hand in hand pretending to be casually chatting. Yasmin had asked their good friend Tony Garcia to be their photographer. She had requested that he take lots of photographs, but her feet were killing her, and she seriously needed to pee. This had to end soon.

"Okay, we're finished the formal photographs." Tony Garcia said, "Unless you can think of something I have forgotten?"

"No!" Replied Carlos, "Er ... I meant, no thank you, Tony. I think you've covered everything for now." He quickly amended.

Yasmin smiled, at Carlos then turned to Tony, "You did a beautiful job, but I need a quick break before we sit down for dinner."

"Si, yes of course." Tony answered.

She caught Jessica's eye, and said, "Baños, help me?"

Jessica nodded, then lightly gripped Yasmin's arm while they walked towards the restrooms. The uneven surfaces and her tight dress made walking in stilettos treacherous. Yasmin could hear Sparky's nails clicking on the tiles as he followed them, probably more out of curiosity than obedience.

Yasmin and Jessica walked side-by-side, taking up most of the space in the hallway leading to the bathrooms. Engrossed in their conversation the sudden appearance of a muscular man dressed in black pants and a white shirt briefly startled them.

"Oh, sorry, I didn't see you," Jessica said.

"Perdón," He held her gaze as he shifted slightly, his body brushing against Jessica's hip.

Concentrating on where she was walking, Yasmin felt Jessica's hand tighten on her arm and heard her mutter, *pendejo* her favourite Spanish curse word. She noticed Sparky lift his nose from his exploration of the sidewalk smells, shifting his attention to Jessica and then to the man.

Inside the women's restroom Yasmin rustled towards the first cubicle.

"Jess, what's wrong?" She asked as she closed the door and caught a glimpse of Jessica's tense frown.

"What a disgusting jerk."

"The waiter that passed us in the hall?" Came the reply from inside the bathroom stall. Yasmin gently tugged her snug dress up to her hips. Having a pee was a bit more complicated than she had envisioned when she and Paloma designed this gorgeous dress.

"Yeah, when he brushed against me I could feel his *woodie*."

"Woodie?"

"A hard-on, a boner, a stiffy. You know, an erection!"

"That is disgusting."

"If I wasn't wearing this long dress I would've kicked him in the *cojones* for being a *pendejo*."

"Jessica!" Yasmin said, "You can't beat up a waiter."

"I will, if he tries that again."

Yasmin burst out laughing. *Yes, Jessica would kick him in the crotch.* "Jess, can you help me with my dress?" She asked, as she flushed the toilet and reached to unlock the cubicle door.

"Sure, come out here where there's more

room."

Yasmin shuffled out, nearly tripping on Sparky.

"Sparky, move out of the way." Jessica pointed her arm at the corner of the room. He grudgingly complied. "Good boy."

"This thing is like a second skin," Jessica joked, straightening and smoothing Yasmin's dress as she tugged it into place. "When are you changing into your other dress?"

"After our first dance together. Then it's time to party!"

"When you are ready Tiff wants start the dinner service. The magicians and the clowns on stilts are keeping the seated guests amused while she and her crew herd the slower ones to their assigned places. Then on her cue we do our grand entrance."

Yasmin laughed, "I can't wait."

Ten minutes later standing just outside the dining area Yasmin and Carlos held hands and smooched.

With a playful grin on her face Tiffany moved to stand in front of the group. "Eve … ry … one rea … dy?" She drawled out.

"Si!" They shouted and the music started. In

a blur of movement and colour the group including Sparky romped into the reception area.

The male lead vocalist of the eight-person band energized the crowd with the familiar lyrics of Pharrell Williams' Happy! "Because I'm happy, clap along if you feel like happiness is the truth, because I'm happy."

The guests obligingly joined in, dancing beside their chairs and singing the popular stuck-in-the-brain-forever lyrics.

Chapter 27

February 22nd Late evening

"Hey you, new guy." The captain of the servers hollered pointing at his newest helper. "Give us a hand."

The new-guy, known as José amongst the crew, hid his cold glare from his temporary boss. Fuentes didn't want to be noticed or remembered. In the last few weeks he had let his hair regrow, changing from his normal close-to-the-skin style and reluctantly removed his plush moustache. Even his distinctive tattoos were covered by the mandatory long-sleeved white shirt. He was just another pair of hands hired for the large event. Anyone could learn to deliver food, refill wine glasses, clear the plates, and be pleasant to the guests.

He strode into the kitchen and was confronted by an enormous white structure. There were five cakes of diminishing sizes stacked one on top of the other. The bottom layer covered most of the space on a table that was at least a metre wide. Their task was to carry everything, the table and the towering confection, out of the kitchen and through the crowd without dropping it. There were three servers gathered around but the leader wanted four men, one holding each side while he kept an eye on the pastry chef's masterpiece.

A few minutes before Fuentes had slipped away from the kitchen, pretending to need a smoke. He walked to the wharf, re-checked that the speedboat was still securely tied at the dock with his version of a quick-release knot. He removed the pistol from under the dashboard, tucking it into his waist band in the small of his back. When the captain of the waiters had told him to help with the cake he quickly slid the pistol behind the empty food boxes stacked beside the kitchen door. His shirt might ride up, revealing the gun while he wrestled with the heavy confection. No point in taking unnecessary chances.

"Oh my goodness! Look at that." Exclaimed a woman pointing at the cake. "It's enormous!"

The head waiter pointed at the centre of the dance floor, indicating this was the final destination. The waiters lowered their burden, tensely watching as the sweet tower swayed slightly right then left. They stepped away leaving their boss to primly smooth the white cloth and adjust the circle of fresh flowers.

Fuentes flicked his gaze around, studying the position of the bridal party. Typically everyone should have been seated in one long row, like a shooting gallery, but this reception was different. The various bridesmaids and groomsmen were casually scattered amongst the guests. They appeared to be seated with their families, and spouses, or dates. The bride and groom were at a central table with both sets of parents. One of the groomsmen had the watchful gaze and the competent vibe of an experienced cop. He was a short distance away from Fuentes' target, but when the shooting started the man would instinctively protect his wife and five youngsters, and deal with the causalities later.

~

"Look up at me, por favor Yasmin," Instructed Tony Garcia, "Perfecto!"

A devious thought made Carlos grin as the tip of the decorated knife slid into the bottom layer of the towering confection. *How mad would she be if I shoved her face in the cake?*

It was a tradition in some parts of Mexico to jokingly push a person's face into their birthday cake, but, this being their wedding day he was certain she would be embarrassed by his prank. His genteel mother-in-law Maria Victoria Guzman de Medina would be horrified. No, better to save that one for a small family gathering a few years down the road and on her actual birthday the 24th of February.

Cameras and phones of every type were pointed at them. Dozens of friends and relatives crowded around for the traditional photographs. He loved this woman with all of his heart, but he was impatient for the formalities to conclude and the zany celebration of their new lives to start.

Finally they were able to sit down again allowing the wait-staff to cut, plate and distribute a piece of cake to each guest. He and Yasmin were the first to be served and he finally comprehended what she had tried to describe to him months ago. Not only were there five large rounds, but inside each one were four layers ranging in colours from deep red to light pink at the top and interspersed with white icing. Using the edge of his fork he cut off a bite and shoved it into his mouth. It was surprising tasty. He wasn't normally impressed by desserts, but this one *took the cake*.

And that pun was so awful it stunk, he mused. He leaned sideways in his chair and put his arm around Yasmin. He kissed her. "Beautiful job, carina."

"Gracias mi amor."

The loud chatter of conversations resumed under-laid with the rattle of plates and the jangle of cutlery. Carlos forked another bite of cake into his mouth and glanced around, checking that everyone was having a good time. Pedro and Maricruz were engrossed in a conversation with Diego and Pedro's sister Cristina. The four Avalos youngsters were playing with Antonio and Luisa Martinez' five youngsters. His siblings Mariana, Nicolas and Roberto plus spouses and offspring occupied two tables. Yasmin's sister Adriana and her husband Enrique plus her two sons, the ring-security guards were nearby.

Once the dancing started the younger ones would find ways to amuse themselves in packs of laughing, shrieking kids. Some would undoubtedly end up playing on the beach or in the water in their party finery. This was what life was about. Family and friends sharing their joy.

Tiffany walked towards them and bent to whisper. "Are you ready for the first dance?"

"Si, of course." Answered Yasmin.

"Let's get this party started." Carlos agreed.

"Good." She straightened up and nodded at the band leader and the beginning notes of *Thinking Out Loud, by Ed Sheeran* began.

Carlos stood and offered Yasmin his hand helping her to her feet.

Lupe Mendoza popped out of her seat. "Momentito, carina," she said straightening the bottom of Yasmin's dress. "Listo! Ready."

"Gracias Mama," Yasmin said, affectionately calling her new mother-in-law, mom.

Carlos led Yasmin to the dance floor and held her close, staring into her deep-green eyes. "I don't deserve you," he whispered, the words catching in his throat and tears sparkling in his eyes.

Her only response was a long slow kiss while they swayed in time to the romantic song.

Fireworks? Carlos pulled away from their embrace and swung his head from looking for the source of the sound. "Did you arrange fireworks for our first dance?" He asked Yasmin.

She opened her mouth to answer, but instead he heard Jessica yelling, and Sparky stridently barking.

Chapter 28

February 22nd Late evening

"Auntie Pattie!" Jessica bellowed, "She's been shot!"

Carlos bounced a glance towards Jessica. Her parents and brothers were beside her. Her mother was a nurse, she would know what to do. He grabbed Yasmin's arm and rapidly towed her away from the dance floor. "Go, hide in the baños!" He said, then pointed at his mother and mother-in-law, "Go with Yasmin. Dad, make sure they are okay."

Raúl Mendoza grimly nodded. "Hurry, just leave your things." He said to his wife Lupe.

Oscar Medina touched his daughter's arm. "Take off your shoes. You can run faster in bare feet."

Yasmin rapidly kicked off the tall-heeled shoes and yanked her dress to calf-height. "Vamos. Let's go." She said, leaving behind her Swarovski crystal-encrusted stilettoes as she ran.

Oscar turned to his wife, Victoria, "Please darling hurry." He made a come-on let's getting moving motion with his hand.

The formidable Victoria Medina wasn't about to be rushed by some mad gunman. She calmly rose and gathered her things and followed the group to the closest ladies' room.

Carlos scanned the room. People shouted, searching for their children and spouses. Some ran crouched-over towards the upper decks. Others ducked under or behind anything that might provide protection. No one knew where the gunman was hiding.

Antonio Martinez, yelled to Luisa, "Get under the table." He reached behind his back and pulled his service Glock. As a captain of the Policía Federal he was allowed to be armed at all times.

"Antonio, find our babies." Luisa demanded. He nodded once to acknowledge her plea.

"Policía! Everyone get down! Now!" Antonio bellowed, as he braced his gun-hand, shoulder height. "Is anyone else injured? Did anyone see the gunman?" The babble of answers indicated that no one had serious injuries, just a few scrapes and bruises, and no one had seen anything.

He swung around in a circle searching for the assailant, shouting instructions as he scanned the crowd. "Diego find an available doctor. Luis call the Red Cross for an ambulance. Pedro contact the policía."

Maricruz shouted, "Antonio, I've already called my commander, he has help on the way. The passenger ferries are just making the last runs for the night, but the *marinas* will search the terminal just in case."

"Bueno," He answered without looking at her. He frantically searched the room looking for any sign of his children. There, Julian his oldest son lifted a table cloth and anxiously peeked at his dad. Antonio quickly released his left hand from his two-handed grip on the Glock, and flashed five fingers at his son and then motioned with his forefinger, *Are all five kids together*?

Julian nodded, and gave his dad a thumbs up.

Antonio motioned Julian to stay hidden.

~

Carlos strode to Jessica's side. "How can I help?"

"Flip that chair over." Anne answered, "I need to prop Pattie up. She ignored the chaos around her. People shouting. Families searching for children. Children crying. Decorations, broken dishes and food crushed underfoot.

"And translate for mom." Jessica replied, as she helped her parents ease Pattie into a semi-sitting position.

Holding a wad of bloody linen napkins pressed tightly to her sister's shoulder she calmly said, "I need more napkins." Her left knee skidded as she shifted her position. It was resting on a squashed piece of cake.

Pattie breathed in short gasps, "How bad, sis?" She asked.

"Just a little scratch, you'll be dancing in an hour or two." Anne joked, as she reached up and took several more napkins from her husband's hand. She felt Gord give her finger-tips a reassuring gentle squeeze. She flashed a quick smile at him then re-focused on her task. "Just lean forward a little bit if you can Pattie, I need to get these in behind your shoulder." A river of blood streamed from the exit wound.

"Ah crap that hurts," Pattie sucked in breath, as her sister pushed the napkins over the wound.

"Lean back against that." Anne instructed, then snuck a quick look at Carlos. "I need a roll of plastic wrap or a couple of clean plastic bags from the kitchen." She shifted her focus back to her sister, "And I need tape, any kind, but duct tape is best."

Carlos turned to the nearest server, asking him if the maintenance man had a storage area. The server relied yes. "We need a roll of heavy-duty tape." He pointed at Jake Sanderson, "Jake can you follow him? I'll stay here with Anne."

"I'm going to wreck your dress, sis." Anne said as she picked up a steak-knife laying nearby and proceeded to slice the dress from Pattie's upper body. "Pretty bra. I'll leave that alone, for now." She teased, trying to side-track her sister's fear.

Carlos pointed at another waiter, and rattled off in Spanish, "Get us a roll of plastic wrap from the kitchen."

"Pneumothorax?" Pattie gasped out the question.

Anne just nodded. Her baby sister was asking if she had what was referred to as a sucking chest wound, a hole that prevent her lung from inflating properly. She and Pattie were both experienced nurses. The situation was life-threatening, but Anne was determined her sister would survive. The plastic film, and tape would seal the wound, helping her sister breathe a little better. They needed medical assistance and quickly.

Jessica said, "She'll have to be transported to Cancun. Our hospital can't deal with critical injuries." She glanced at Sparky, checking he was still nearby. He was intently smelling the floor near the wedding cake. *That's odd, he doesn't scrounge food*. And then her thoughts ricocheted back to her aunt's dire situation.

"Jess, we'll use our boat." Pedro piped up, searching the crowd for his brother-in-law. "I'll grab Diego, and be back as quickly as possible."

"Any luck locating a doctor?" She asked.

"Doctora Marion is nearby and she should be here in a few minutes."

Carlos looked for Antonio, "Tony, what's the situation? Do you think we are safe to get people moving?"

"Yes, I did a quick look around and as far as I can tell there was only one gunman." Antonio, holstered his pistol and walked towards the group. "I instructed the manager to get guests out as quickly and as orderly as possible. We don't want a traffic jam in the parking lot with panicky people smashing into each other's cars."

Jake and the waiter returned almost simultaneously with the requested duct tape and plastic wrap. Jake knelt by his mother and aunt,

"How big a piece mom?" He asked, holding up the box of kitchen wrap.

"About a foot, then fold it into a square. I'll need two pieces for the front and the back."

Jessica took the roll of tape from the waiter and ripped off a piece that was longer than the square of plastic. "When you are ready, the tape is to your right, Mom," She said, as she held it by one corner and dangled it near her mother.

Jake handed her the first piece and Anne removed the linen napkins, holding the plastic tightly against Pattie's body. "Jess you stick it on while I hold it steady."

They repeated the process for the other three sides of the square. "Now comes the fun part, Pattie. I'm going to have to tilt you a little forward and apply the patch to the exit wound." She gave her sister a reassuring smile.

Pattie groaned and reached to squeeze Matt's hand while Anne and Jessica worked on sealing the wound in her back.

Barefoot and her dress yanked up past her knees, Yasmin hurried to join the group. "Oh, my God." She exclaimed, as her hands flew up to her mouth. "What happened?"

"Auntie Pattie has been shot." Jessica said. Tears trickled down her face as she applied the last piece of duct tape.

"The ambulance and a doctor have just arrived." Luis hollered from the front entrance.

"We need oxygen. Immediately." Anne shouted back, as she studied her sister's pallid face. Pattie was still losing blood, and she was having difficulties breathing. "Hang on sis," She said, smiling at Pattie. "You can do this."

Pattie held her sister's gaze and whispered, "Look after my Riley." She said referring to her fourteen-year-old dog. "He's too old to re-home with strangers."

"Stop talking nonsense, Pattie." Anne retorted. "You'll be fine, and Riley needs you."

Chapter 29

February 22nd Midnight

Fuentes bumped the speedboat against the private dock on the Cancun side of the bay. He let the motor idle, pushing the bow against the wharf while he hopped off and secured the forward line then quickly tied off the stern line. He reached in and flicked off the ignition.

The night had turned into a monumental screw-up. That *pinche* woman had leaned forwards at exactly the wrong moment. He didn't wait to see if she was dead. He had quickly taken another shot at Jessica Sanderson and ran. He had heard an explosion of glass and crockery. She had yelled for help for her aunt, but not for herself. He had likely missed her entirely. Not the outcome he wanted.

The question was would Fernandez see tonight as a success? Or a failure? He chewed on that thought for a moment. *Failure.* He only had two options. Move to another country. Or, finish the job.

He would update his boss later, in the meantime he had a few things to organize. He swiped the screen of his disposable phone, and thumbed in a number.

"Bueno?" Asked a wary voice.

"No names, this isn't my regular number." he warned his younger brother Matías.

"Claro."

"Take your family and leave now. Don't tell me where you are going."

"Problemos?"

"Si, if you don't hear from me in a week, take everything." He was telling his brother to access his bank account and take the money. Alfonso trusted his brother enough to give him a debit card for the account and Matías had done the same for him.

They were the two remaining siblings in a family of five boys and one girl. The Fuentes family had lost heavily by being involved in a criminal lifestyle. Even their parents were dead. Live hard, die young and have a good-looking corpse was a grim joke shared by the brothers.

"Te amo," Matías replied, telling his brother he loved him.

"Lo mismo, the same," Fuentes said, thinking this might be the last time that he spoke to his remaining sibling. "Te amo, adios."

He pulled the battery and tossed the cheap device into the ocean. He had three more still in their boxes in the trunk of his car.

His next call would be to his contact on Isla Mujeres. Fuentes strode up the ramp to the parking lot, pointed his remote control at his car and popped the trunk open. He selected a box containing a new cellphone. He stuffed the battery into the slot then powered up the cheap device. He punched the numbers from memory.

Chapter 30

February 23rd After midnight

"Just a little higher," Jessica said, "and it'll clear the railing." She straightened her arms, helping the Red Cross attendants lift Pattie and the stretcher onto the back deck of the *Bruja del Mar*. Sparky paced near her feet.

Diego and Pedro had commandeered a waiter and his car to drive them around Sac Bajo, the finger of land on the western side of the Laguna Makax, where Zama's Beach Club and several other beach resorts were located. It was frustrating. The *Bruja del Mar* was visible from the small dock in the lagoon where the pangas had dropped off the guests a few hours ago, but without another boat it was only accessible by driving around the inlet. Once they reached their destination the men had rapidly powered up the big yacht and pounded out of the marina, back to the bigger wharf on ocean-side of Zama's Beach Club. It was the same wharf where the yacht had docked disgorging the joyous group a few hours before.

The unavoidable delay to transport Pattie Packard was maddening, but at this time of night a private vessel was the only option for getting her to a Cancun hospital.

Jessica could see both Carlos and Yazmin trying to help lift the stretcher but there were already enough helpers. Matt and Jake stood mid-distance, one on each side of the metal cot keeping their aunt balanced. As the stretcher moved over the railing one attendant shifted his grip to the handles by her head, keeping the portable bed as level and stable as possible. Diego grabbed the grips at the foot of the bed.

Sparky zipped aboard the boat, dashing up the narrow gangplank while the group wrestled her aunt's stretcher over the railing. Jessica didn't call him back. He liked boats. He would behave.

Jessica had seen Carlos' friend, Captain Antonio Martinez, coordinating with the local policía and the Navy to secure the scene and to search for the gunman. Cristina Avalos and Luisa Martinez had gathered up their combined families and gone to the Avalos' home. Carlos' parents, siblings and their families were headed to his house. Yasmin's family said they were returning to their hotel rooms. The youngsters would soon fall asleep, but the adults would be anxiously waiting to hear how Pattie was doing.

Jessica noticed that while the doctor stabilized her aunt at the venue, Yasmin had somehow managed to change into her shorter dress. She insisted on going to Cancun with them but she had difficulties walking in the long, snug-fitting bridal dress so she had swapped clothes. Jessica and Maricruz had shortened their long gowns by pulling the excess above their knees and securing it with a collection safety pins and twist-ties scrounged from the kitchen.

It was terrible that Carlos and Yasmin's wedding had been ruined, but all she cared about right now was the survival of her aunt. *Why the hell had someone shot her? It just didn't make any sense.*

"Doctora, will a Red Cross ambulance meet us on the Cancun side?" Anne asked as they eased away from the Zama's dock.

"I was told there is a thirty-minute wait for an available Red Cross vehicle." The doctor said while re-checking Pattie's vital signs, "I've already contacted a private company. It will cost more, but be much quicker."

"Thank you." Anne answered. "Time is more critical than cost."

"They'll be at the dock when we arrive." Doctora Marion assured her.

The two Red Cross attendants disembarked the boat, leaving a few supplies for Doctora Marion should she need them. They had explained they were short-handed and couldn't leave the island. Even just not having the stretcher available for an unknown period of time was a hardship for the small unit.

Anne lightly squeezed Pattie's hand. "You hang in there sis. No bailing out on me."

Jessica saw the grim expression in her mother's eyes when Pattie's eyelids barely fluttered. *Please, please, please.* She silently begged any deity, of any religion, that might be listening.

Diego said, "Pedro, Maricruz, and I will wait on the boat."

"It's a private dock. Won't they tell you to leave?" Carlos asked.

"We know one of the company managers. We've done a few favours for him," Pedro said. "He's told the security guards we can stay as long as necessary."

"Why don't you just go back to the island?" Jessica asked, as she repeatedly stroked Sparky's head.

"The passenger ferries won't start up again until five o'clock. You might need a ride before then," Diego replied quietly, his sad eyes holding her gaze. "We'll wait at the Ultramar gas dock."

Jessica's heart skittered when she realized what he was hinting at. *No!* They would have a long and stressful night sitting in the emergency ward, but she refused to consider any outcome except her Aunt Pattie's survival and eventual recovery. They would not return to the island, leaving her aunt's body alone in the cold morgue.

Her brother Matt sat beside her and wrapped an arm around her shoulders. She tucked an arm around his waist, as he leaned against her. Neither of them spoke. Her free hand reached for the comfort of Sparky's compact body, pulling him tight against her other leg.

Chapter 31

February 23rd After mid-night

"Antonio Martinez, Policía Federal Mexico City," He said flashing his police identification at the local commander. "I'm a guest at this *boda*."

The municipal Comandante de Policía lifted his chin and belligerently eyed Martinez. "We've met before. You have a habit of causing trouble on our peaceful little island."

"Si, I remember you as well." Antonio smiled, holding eye contact with the man as his brain spun through names. *Julian Camara. Si. That was his name*. "A pleasure to see you again, Comandante Camara." He held out his hand but the other man ignored the gesture, and Antonio let his hand drop slowly back to his side.

Okay then, that's how it's going to be. Antonio pulled his lips into a tight line to keep his amusement from sneaking into his expression. The man was apparently still angry about a past incident that ended with the death of an American.

The dead *pendejo* was a nasty serial killer and his demise was no great loss to the gene pool, but, he was a foreigner and his death had created a pile of paperwork for the local policía. Plus even though his position in the Policía Federal trumped the local commander's he had been operating on the man's turf, without advising him. That was big no-no in their regimented world.

"I grew up here with Carlos Mendoza, Diego Avalos and Pedro Velazquez. I was one of the groomsmen." Antonio said, trying to connect with Camara. The big difference Antonio had noticed since his last visit to the island was most of the municipal cops wore a pistol strapped to their thighs. In Mexico the local cops were typically not armed, similar to the British police. In the past only the specialist teams were trained and authorized to carry firearms. It was a sign of the times he supposed; more problems and more guns.

Camara made a dismissive sound, sucking on his front teeth. "What happened here?" He pointed at the mess with his chin.

"One injured, Canadian woman, mid-fifties, through and through gunshot to the shoulder. She is in serious condition and was transported via personal boat to Cancun. I am waiting for an update from the family." He said, repeating his report again. It was standard police procedure;

start with the first-on-the-scene and work your way up to the person with the jazzy decorations on the shoulder-boards and the fancy hat. "Victim's name is Pattie Packard, related to local resident Jessica Sanderson who is one of the bridal party."

"Jessica Sanderson. I know that name. She's a problem, just like you."

Martinez wisely remained silent. No sense *poking the bear* just yet. It was advantageous to keep the local boss as calm as possible while he searched for evidence.

"It looks like it was quite a party," Camara said. Antonio could hear a hint of envy in his voice.

"Si, a lot of preparation went into this celebration for my good friends."

Antonio swept his gaze over the remnants of what had been the beginnings of an all-night celebration for two of his favourite people. There had been a lot of fun entertainment planned for the evening. Besides the eight-person band, and the mariachis, he had noticed two clowns on stilts, a spinning cage for disco dancers, and a werewolf holding a large funny picture frame. There were glow-in-the-dark glasses and carnival masks stacked on a nearby counter ready for a night of silly fun. Everything was set to go as soon as the romantic first dance was finished.

Then shots were fired, and the party preparations went all to hell. People grabbed spouses and children, scrambling to find what they hoped would be a safe hiding place. Dishes were broken, wine glasses smashed, and desserts trampled in their haste to find safety. As it turned out only two shots were fired, and one person seriously injured. Antonio was certain the wrong person was shot. He had a hunch that Jessica might be the intended target. She had a habit of finding trouble.

"Any suspects?" Camara asked. His eyes skipped past Antonio's, scanning the room.

"None that I know of." He lied. Camara had been rude, and now he wanted Antonio to solve his case for him. Two could play this game. He had one small titbit of information that he had kept to himself. The head-waiter had said that he had several new-hires working the event. Everyone was still there helping to clean up the mess, except one waiter. His name was José Lopez, as common a name as John Smith in English. He also had a vague description of the missing man. It wasn't much, but it was a start.

"Huh." Camara grunted a reply. His gaze was now focused on a spot over Antonio's left shoulder.

Martinez turned his head and curbed a laugh. The man was staring at the dessert bar still heaped with trays of cookies, slices, and brownies. "Por favor, help yourself Comandante. It will just be given to the staff or thrown out." Antonio swept an arm towards the display, inviting the other man to help himself.

"Gracias," Camara said over his shoulder as he walked towards the goodies.

Chapter 32

February 23rd After mid-night

Sergeant Felipe Ramirez of the Isla Mujeres Municipal police scrutinized the interaction between Antonio Martinez, and his boss Comandante Julian Camara. He read suppressed anger in the body language of Martinez. Camara displayed indifference. He was busy stuffing his face with sweets.

Ramirez could guess what Camara's assessment would be. *The tourist bought drugs from the wrong person, then bad things happened. Case closed.*

Only casual acquaintances until recently, Ramirez and Diego had become good friends because of Jessica Sanderson and her trouble-finding beach mutt. Comandante Camara had one thing right. Isla Mujeres was normally peaceful and had a very low crime rate, but recently whenever there was a problem the good-looking blonde and her pooch seemed to be in the middle of the mess.

Ramirez and his partner Constable Alexis Gomez had been invited to *la boda*, the wedding, but they were scheduled to work and couldn't find anyone who would switch shifts. Alexis was still bitching and moaning about not being able to attend what she said was the social event of the year. He just wished he had been here when Jessica's aunt was shot. Perhaps between them and Martinez they could have captured the assailant. Ramirez locked eyes with Antonio's, then tilted his chin in the direction of the docks. *Meet me outside.*

Antonio nodded and moved towards the exit.

Ramirez flicked a glance at his boss, ensuring the man was still concentrating on the sweets then followed Martinez outside.

"Good to see you," Antonio said, giving his friend a back-slap guy-hug.

"You too." Felipe replied. "I wish I'd been here to help."

"It was quick, too fast to do anything. I think the gunman was a pro."

"But a middle-aged Canadian woman? Why?"

Martinez scratched his eyebrow, "I think Jessica was the target. According to one of her nephews the aunt leaned forward to say something and probably just got in the way."

"It's a possibility, I suppose," Ramirez studied Antonio face for a moment, thinking.

Antonio pressed on, "Jessica and Sparky found the murdered taxi driver. And she helped *Teniente* Zapata capture that low-level drug dealer. My federal sources told me both incidents were connected to Rafael Fernandez, a drug cartel boss. That's why I think she was the target."

"Si, you could be right," Ramirez conceded, remembering a guarded call in September from Detective Dante Toledo of the State Police, warning him to watch his back. His connection with Diego and friends could lead to trouble for Ramirez. Toledo had said *Don* Rafael was enraged and that he wanted payback.

"You have any ideas?"

"One of the servers is my cousin." Ramirez said meaning the man was related to him in some vague way. In Mexico the word cousin had many meanings; childhood friend, first cousin, or twenty-seventh-cousin-once-removed. It didn't matter, they were all considered cousins. He pointed at the wharf, "My cousin told me a waiter docked a small speedboat earlier in the afternoon. He said he lived in Cancun, and this was a quick and cheap way to commute for work. After the shooting the boat was gone."

"Any description?"

"Average size, average height. Brown, brown and brown." Ramirez answered, meaning brown hair, brown eyes, and possibly Latino.

"I asked Pepe the head-waiter about his staff. He said everyone except one person, José Lopez, was still here. Vague description. No moustache. Medium length hair. Fit."

"Anything else?" Asked Ramirez.

"He was one of the waiters carrying in the cake according to Pepe." Then Antonio snapped his fingers, "Photos! Tony Garcia took photos. The cake was huge. It took four men to carry it. I'm sure I saw Tony taking pictures."

"Is he still here?"

"No, he and Betsy left soon after the shooting."

Ramirez checked his contact list. "I have Tony's number. Hopefully they aren't asleep." He said.

"Well?" Antonio demanded when Ramirez ended the call.

"Tony has about a thousand photos. As soon as he can locate the ones of the waiters carrying the cake he's going to send them to my email."

"Let's hope he got a good one of the four waiters."

Ramirez heard a soft ping, and checked his phone. He flicked the screen to open the message. "Photos. That was fast." He swore softly, "Damn this tiny screen. It's hard to see, but I think Tony got some good photos. I need a computer to have a better look."

"Maybe I can pick him out." Antonio said, leaning closer to the images. "No, too small. Send them to me. I have an iPad back at the hotel."

"Done."

"Good," Antonio said, as he heard the ping of an incoming message, "Are you going to tell Camara about the photos?"

Ramirez shifted his feet, "Later."

Antonio gave him a knowing look. "Claro."

Ramirez heard a loud ringtone off to his right. He turned his head and glanced at the rookie constable. The man sheepishly answered and turned his body away, whispering. *Probably his girlfriend checking up on him.*

~

"Bueno."

"Do you recognize my voice?" Fuentes demanded.

"Si."

"I need information."

"I'm at the scene of the shooting," The man whispered, "I can't talk now."

"I don't give a damn. Find out which hospital she was taken to, and the status." Fuentes snarled at his police informer. "Call me back in exactly ten minutes." He disconnected and removed the battery, checking the time on his watch.

At nine minutes he reinserted the battery, and fifty seconds later it rang. "Si."

"At the Amerimed, in the Plaza las Americas. Serious condition, but expected to live." Came the guarded answer.

"And the family?"

"In the waiting room."

"How many?"

"Eight in total. Three more are waiting on the *Bruja*, at the Ultramar dock."

"Keep your phone on." Fuentes demanded and disconnected the call. He again removed the battery, shoving it and the cellular deep inside a pocket.

Eleven people at two locations. He couldn't attempt to kill them without at least four more gunmen. Two with him to hit the hospital and two to hit the boat. The assassinations which might include medical staff as collateral damage would cause wide-spread panic in the tourist industry. Exactly what he advised *Don* Rafael not to do.

Jessica Sanderson was the un-official ringleader of their group of friends. It had been his idea to kill her as a warning to the others to keep their noses out of Rafael Fernandez's businesses.

She had to die, tonight. Or, very soon he would be dead.

~

"This is all my fault," Jessica murmured as she shifted in the rigid molded-plastic chair.

"What are you talking about?" Yasmin gripped Jessica's hand.

"I insisted that she come to your wedding." She turned her tear-stained face to Yasmin, "If she dies, it will be because of me."

"No, the only person responsible is the *pendejo* who pulled the trigger!" Yasmin retorted.

"She's right, Jessie," Anne said.

Jessica didn't respond she just stared across the waiting room at her mom. She was rigidly erect in a hard plastic chair. Her dress, her shoes, and her hands were painted with her sister's blood. There was a streak of red on her forehead where she had tried to wipe a stray piece of hair out of her eyes. Stuck to one knee was a big glob of pink cake and white icing.

"There's no one to blame but the asshole who did this."

Jessica's throat clogged with emotion. She guiltily looked away from her mom and concentrated on her family and friends. Her dad paced. Jessica could hear the slap of his shoes, back and forth, back and forth. She knew he loved his sister-in-law, as if she was his own baby sister. She had never seen her dad so agitated. Typically, whenever they had to wait, her dad and brothers would try to snatch a few minutes of rest. It was a first-responders habit, nap whenever possible. Their jobs changed from relaxed and joking to crisis-response with the call-out alarm, with no time to even take a leak.

Her gaze slid to the other side of the room where Matt and Jake were propped in chairs too small for their long bodies. Their lengthy femurs stretched forward as they balanced their asses on the edge of the seat. Their heads rested against a painted wall, left smudged and dirty by previous occupants of those same chairs. Both men had their right ankle crossed over the left, and their hands comfortably resting in their laps. Except for the difference in hair and eye colour they could be twins.

Jessica noticed Carlos shift from one side of his ass to the other and back again, trying to restore the circulation in his legs. In her experience all waiting rooms were damn uncomfortable. It was as if the designers deliberately created an atmosphere of discomfort to add to the anxiety and stress.

Half-listening to a conversation between her parents Jessica heard her mom ask a question. "Didn't you think it was a little odd that you had to get cash from the ATM for the other ambulance?" Anne said.

"I have to admit," Gord answered, "I was a bit worried when the ambulance driver asked me to walk across that dark street to the bank ATM, and take out money to pay for their services."

"Why did you have to do that?" Jessica pulled herself upright, and cocked an eyebrow at her dad. She had seen him walking across the double-wide boulevard with the driver, but hadn't paid much attention to what he was doing.

"Because it was a catered event with an open bar, we only brought a little bit of cash with us." Gord fanned his hand at his sons and wife. "We didn't have enough money between us to pay them."

"Oh, Dad, I had no idea," Jessica said. "I wouldn't have been any help either. All I have is a bit of makeup in my tiny bag."

"Me too," said Yasmin.

Carlos turned out his empty pockets, "Gord asked me, and I said I had nothing on me. Everything had been prepaid."

"Wouldn't they take a credit card? Or a debit card?" Asked Jessica.

"Sure, but their little portable card-reader wasn't working so we had to try the ATM."

"What the hell would we have done if that hadn't worked?"

"No idea." Gord said to the suddenly quiet group.

Chapter 33

February 23rd Before sunrise

"Hola Diego." Jessica said. "Auntie Pattie is just out of surgery. Doctora Marion says she's stable."

"*Gracias a Dios*." Diego replied, "Are you staying? Or coming back to the island? We are still waiting at the ferry dock with the *Bruja*."

"Just a minute," Jessica moved her phone away from her ear and studied her mother. "Mom, do you want to head back to the island to sleep for a few hours? Maybe have a shower and change your clothes?" She asked pointing at the blood-soaked dress her mother still wore.

"I don't want to leave Pattie," Her mother replied. "You go ahead. I'm fine."

Jessica's eyes swung to Gord. "How about you Dad?"

"I'll stay here with your mom. You go ahead, get cleaned up and bring her a change of clothes."

Yasmin spoke up, "Jess, Doctora Marion just went to ask the nurses if there is a shower that your family can use. The bigger facilities usually have an area where visitors can clean up."

"Sis, why don't you and everyone else head back to the island? I'll stay with Mom and Dad." Jake said, "When you get back, I'll go."

"Diego, are you still there?" Jessica spoke into her iPhone.

"Si, I've been listening." He answered.

"Some of us will come back to the island with you. Some will stay. We'll sort it out and be there as soon as possible. Okay?"

"Si, claro." He said, and disconnected.

Doctora Marion returned. "There is a bathroom, with a shower that anyone can use." She pointed down the hall past the nurses' station.

"Thank you, Doctora," Gord said.

"I'm going back to Isla, to get out of this dress and to get clean clothes for Mom and Dad. Diego, Pedro and Maricruz are waiting for us on the boat." Jessica said, "But, Carlos, I have a favour to ask. Would you wait here with my parents to translate for them while the rest of us dash back to the island? We'll come back as quickly as we can."

"Si, of course, of course." He replied.

"I'll stay with you, mi amor," Added Yasmin.

"*Carina* I'm fine." He said, "Go home, and sleep if you can."

Anne spoke up, "Everyone, please, go back to Isla. Get cleaned up, put on comfy clothes, eat a meal and come back when you are ready. Gord and I will be fine on our own for a few hours." She put one arm around Jessica and gave her a reassuring squeeze, "I'm an old hand at this stuff sweetie. Don't worry about me."

Jessica was about to object when a nurse approached the group, "Señora Sanderson I have some clean pyjamas for you." She said in very clear English. "You should have a shower and put on fresh things. It will make you feel better."

Anne reached for the pile of pale blue hospital-issue sleepwear. "Thank you so much, at least you didn't give me the open-back nightie to wear." She smiled tiredly at the woman. "My sister, Pattie, and I are both nurses in Canada."

"Si, la doctora told me," The nurse pointed at Doctora Marion. "We will take very good care of your sister."

"Gracias."

Jessica chewed her lower lip, and studied her parents. She knew their knowledge of the Spanish language was limited to thank you, please, and how to ask where the bathroom was by saying *baños* with a question in their voice. "Mom," She asked, "are you sure?"

"Yes, that nurse speaks English. We'll manage. Come back when you're rested."

"I'll stay with your parents," Doctora Marion said, "I am fluent in both languages, including the Spanish equivalent of medical jargon." She added with a small smile.

Jessica's gaze swung again to her dad, he nodded in agreement with her mom. She glanced at Jake, and then at Matt. They both smiled faintly and shrugged their wide shoulders. Her family knew it was pointless to argue with their iron-willed mother once she had made up her mind.

"Okay, then let's get going. The sooner we get cleaned up the quicker we can get back here." Jessica pressed the *last call* icon on her phone. "Hola Diego. We're on our way."

~

Fuentes eased his Yamaha Road Star 1700 motorcycle into a shadowy space alongside the parking-ramp at the ferry terminal. He had driven his white Jeep back to a storage unit that no one, not even *Don* Rafael, knew about. He had exchanged the car for the big motorcycle. It was fast and nimble. It was perfect for a quick escape.

The all-black bike was unremarkable unless a Road Star enthusiast happened to spot it. He thought the odds of that happening were pretty low.

He flipped the kick stand into position and slung his right leg off the bike onto the ground. He reached to the small of his back, checking his gun was still secure. Fuentes casually glanced around. A handful of sleepy commuters were purchasing tickets then lining-up for the first passenger boat to the island. He spotted a bench in the shadows near the OXXO convenience store and sat. His left arm comfortably rested on the back of the seat, his right ankle was propped on his left knee. Leaning back into the shadows, he waited.

Judging by the tremor in the rookie cop's voice, Fuentes was certain he would be noticeably nervous if he called him again tonight. He didn't want a suspicious supervisor asking his informant difficult questions. Instead he had called his contact at the hospital.

The young nurses' aide was another greedy person blinded by the promise of easy money. She had reported that most of the group were returning to the island, via the private boat that had brought them to the mainland. She had been listening to their conversations, and even though she only spoke Spanish she understood enough English to figure out their plans. The woman said the five younger people, three men and two women had left the older couple and the *doctora* at the hospital. The security guard had arranged for two taxis to pick the others up at the front entrance.

The headlights of two vehicles turning into the drop-off area caught Fuentes eye. He eased his foot back to the ground and leaned forward. Remaining as still as a sniper, his eyes flicked from car to car searching for his prey.

"Jess, over here!" Boomed a voice, just as Jessica Sanderson's foot touched the pavement.

Fuentes flicked his gaze in the direction of the voice. A stocky Maya was being towed by a dog that lunged excitedly towards the taxis. *Mierda! The guy called Pedro and that mutt Sparky*!

"Sparky, baby! I forgot about you." Jessica levered her way out of the taxi and squatted, waiting for her dog to run into her arms.

In a fluid blur of motion Fuentes stood and pulled his pistol. Sparky snapped his head around and lunged, ripping his leash from Pedro's hands. The dog sprinted straight at Fuentes.

Fuentes fired a shot at Jessica, then her dog. The first shot shattered the taxi window. The second shot bounced off the concrete as the dog sunk his teeth into Fuentes' calf muscle. Cursing Fuentes ran towards his motorcycle dragging the tenacious dog. He kicked the dog in the head to dislodge his fangs, and swung his injured leg over the saddle. He cranked the throttle to maximum power. The tires screamed in protest as he blasted out onto the street. Something hard bounced off his head. Stunned, he swerved and the bike wobbled. He gunned the engine and regained control, evading the enraged men chasing his motorcycle.

Zigging and zagging through the light morning traffic, he raced back to his secret storage unit. He wheeled the bike inside, and slumped onto the floor.

His head pounded and blood dripped on his shoulder. His leg was on fire from the deep puncture wounds, and the flesh was torn when he had kicked the dog loose. He couldn't get a good aim to kill it while dragging it towards the motorcycle. He was more concerned with escaping

Local motorcycle riders seldom used protective clothing or helmets. Isla Mujeres had a helmet law that was somewhat enforced, but Cancun didn't.

Now, he wished he had worn both the leathers and the brain-bucket.

Chapter 34

February 23rd Sunrise

"Sparky!" Jessica ran to her dog. "No, please, not you too." At the sound of her panicky voice Sparky tried to lift his head, then sagged back to the pavement. The tip of his tail fluttered twice, and then stilled. She hiked up the dark-blue bridesmaid's dress that just a few hours before had been stunningly beautiful. It was tattered, torn, speckled with her auntie's blood, and now dirty from kneeling next to her sweet furry friend. *It was just a damn dress. Sparky was her very best friend in the world.*

Jake trotted back to their location red-faced and sweating. He had chased the motorcycle rider through the parkade but lost him as the biker sped in and out of the traffic. Matt was about a dozen steps behind him, his chest heaving with exertion.

"The bastard's gone, but I clobbered him in the head." Jake said, he leaned forward resting his hands on his knees and breathed heavily. "I spotted a baseball-sized piece of concrete and pitched it at him."

"I wish you had knocked him off the bike, and then a big truck had run him over. Twice!" Jessica snapped.

"Yeah, me too," Jake agreed. "Are you okay, sis?"

"Fabulous! Just freaking fabulous!" She snapped. "I have to get Sparky to a vet, immediately."

"I know a clinic that's open all-hours, Jess. I'll go with you." Pedro said, then added, "Carlos, can you give Diego a hand taking the *Bruja* back to Isla?"

Carlos said, "Sure, no problem." Then he pointed at Maricruz, "And we have Teniente Zapata with us. We'll be fine."

Yasmin hurried towards the group, "I stopped a taxi on the street. It'll be here in a minute or two. The driver is just turning his car around and coming in through the vehicle entrance."

"Will he take a dog?" Asked Matt.

Yasmin quirked a tired smile, "I did the damsel in distress thing, and I offered him double the fare. He'll do it."

Despite the tense situation, Jessica smiled briefly. She could picture her beautiful friend turning the full force of her gorgeous green eyes on the vulnerable taxi driver. "Love you, *seesta*," She said, using their humorous code-name.

"Love you more." Yasmin responded, lightly hugging Jessica.

~

Standing beside the examination table at the veterinary clinic Jessica gently touched Sparky's paw. The veterinarian attached an x-ray of Sparky's head and neck to a wall-mounted light box. Then he pointed at different areas and spoke in rapid Spanish. Jessica could make out an occasional word, but he was speaking too quickly for her dead-tired brain to make much sense of his assessment.

Finally Pedro turned to her and translated. "Doctor Cupul says he doesn't see any broken bones. Sparky's jaw and neck look fine. None of his teeth are missing or loose. The blood work looks okay. But there is still the possibility of a concussion."

"Why is he so still?" Asked Jessica.

Pedro translated to the doctor, and then to Jessica.

"He thinks Sparky has a massive headache or whiplash. The doctor is going to give him a shot for pain." Pedro said, then added. "Just in case he has a concussion the doc wants to keep him under observation for a day or two."

"I can't leave my boy here on his own."

"It's the right decision, Jess." Pedro gently put his arm around Jessica, "You have enough on your plate with your Auntie Pattie. You can't nurse an injured dog too. It's better for him to stay here."

"Si, I know," Jessica wiped her eyes, then gave Pedro a fierce hug. "Love you, *mi hermano*." She said, calling him brother; an expression of affection among close friends. "You saved my life."

"Not me," Pedro said. "He saved you," He said pointing at Sparky.

"Yes, you're right. He did. He attacked that *pendejo* before we even knew he was a threat." She smiled at Sparky, and lightly touched his shoulder. "What made you do that little man?" She asked. His only response was a slight movement of his tail.

"I've been wondering the same thing." Pedro said, "It's as if he instinctively knew he was *el hombre malo*. A bad guy."

Jessica pulled at her bottom lip with her thumb and forefinger, as her brain replayed the incident when the waiter deliberately brushed against her body. "I've seen him before."

"Where?"

"At the reception. Yasmin and I were headed to the ladies' room before dinner and he was in the hallway leading to the *baños*."

"What made you notice him?"

"Because he rubbed up against me and he had an erection!" She snorted. "I hadn't been wearing this dress I'd have given him a good hard kick in the *cojones*."

Pedro burst out laughing, causing the veterinary to look at him with a puzzled expression. He explained Jessica's comments to the doctor who grinned and pretended to protect his *cojones* with both hands while muttering *una mujer muy peligrosa*.

"The doctor says you are a very dangerous woman." Pedro translated.

"Yeah, I got that."

"Your incident with the waiter still doesn't explain why Sparky attacked him, unless you've trained him to bite anybody who annoys you."

"No ... but that's a good idea," She said, pretending to consider his suggestion then added, "While Mom and I were working on Auntie Pattie's wounds I noticed Sparky investigating the floor around the cake-table and the route to the kitchen. Maybe this time he recognized the man's smell and instinctively knew he was dangerous."

"He does have an amazing ability to find things and people with that extraordinary nose of his."

"He has a nose for finding trouble." She agreed wryly.

"Doctor Cupul suggests we leave. He'll take good care of your boy." Pedro said, listening and translating almost simultaneously. "He says you have to take care of yourself, too. He can see you are very tired and stressed."

"I am tired, but I still have to get Mom a clean set of clothes and change out of this wreckage." She said flipping a hand at her dress.

"Okay, say goodbye to The Sparkinator and let's get going."

"The Sparkinator! I love that." Jessica lowered her voice and said, "I'll be back," imitating movie tough-guy Arnold Schwarzenegger's famous line from Terminator 2.

"Love you little man." She gave Sparky a light kiss on his head. "Please get better."

~

On the Ultramar passenger ferry Pedro was glad Jessica had quickly dozed off, her head resting against his shoulder. It was only an eighteen minute boat ride, but it was better than no sleep at all.

Pedro relaxed into the seat and closed his eyes, hoping for a bit of shut-eye himself, instead a continuous loop of images ran though his brain. The shooting of Pattie Packard. The rush to get the boat and to transport her to Cancun. Waiting on the boat with Diego, Maricruz and Sparky. It had been a fluke that Sparky wanted a pee break about the time that Jessica and the others arrived at the terminal. He couldn't believe how lucky she had been — twice.

He would be devastated if she had been injured, or killed. They had been close friends since she had moved to Isla and even though he was attracted to her, theirs wasn't a romantic relationship.

He sometimes wondered if the timing had been different would she be interested in him. When they met he was in a long-term relationship with Camila Gomez, until she left him for a man from Mexico City. He hadn't seen the breakup coming and it hurt him deeply. By the time he could cope with Camila's unexpected departure Jessica was involved with Luis Aguilar. And now the vivacious and tough Teniente Maricruz Zapata had entered his life. *The randomness of life.*

Pedro felt the boat slow as it neared their destination and he opened his eyes. Jessica's mouth was hanging slightly open as she breathed deeply. He suppressed the childish urge to sneak a photo and post it on Instagram. She would be angry as hell if he did.

Instead he nudged her, "Hey, Sleeping Beauty. Wake up."

Chapter 35

February 23rd Late afternoon

Dressed in non-descript jeans, loose shirts, and scuffed footwear four men hunched over a wobbly red plastic table in a Cancun family-style taqueria. Each man had a cup of strong coffee and the remnants of a hearty meal in front of them. This was an unofficial gathering and Martinez had suggested they dress-down, to blend with the regular clientele of the café.

Even though Martinez and Ramirez had only snatched a few hours of sleep, they had arranged a meet-up with Detectives Marco Cervera and Dante Toledo. The four cops had agreed to share their information and not get into a pissing contest over who was in charge.

The four men had figured out a strong connection between the young Cuban females and the drug kingpin Rafael Fernandez — the seemingly untouchable man controlling the Cancun human-trafficking, sex-slave, and drug-distribution. Their main objective was to end his reign of fear, torture, and executions. Their secondary goal was to find the *pendejo* who had twice tried to kill Antonio's friend, Jessica Sanderson.

Antonio Martinez propped his iPad on the table, and flicked to the photos that Tony Garcia had supplied. He stopped on the image of the waiters struggling to carry the gigantic cake. "Earlier today I showed this to my friends. Jessica said this is the dude that rubbed his stiffy against her as she and Yasmin were headed to the baños." He indicated a man in the picture.

Martinez guffawed when he saw the questioning expression on Toledo's face. "You've never met the impressive Señorita Sanderson." He grinned, "She's gorgeous, self-reliant, and tough."

"She told me she would have kicked him in the *cojones,* but couldn't because of her long dress." Ramirez added, "I wouldn't mess with her." The uh-uh-not-me look on his face elicited rough laughs from the others.

Still looking puzzled, Toledo interjected, "But now she can identify him."

"He was going to kill her," Martinez flatly stated, "Rubbing against her probably cranked his motor."

Grunts of agreement then a momentary lull in the conversation followed that statement.

"Anybody know this dirt bag's name?" Martinez asked, pointing again at the same image.

Cervera nodded, "I think that's Alfonso Fuentes. He's the right-hand man for Fernandez." Marco replied. "Do you have any better photos of him?"

"No, but I can enlarge the image," Martinez touched the screen and swept his thumb and forefinger apart. "Better?"

Cervera leaned closer and studied the screen, "Si, definitely Fuentes. No moustache. Longer hair. But that's him."

"Bueno," Martinez said, "Now we have another tie-in with Fernandez."

"Anything new on the boat captain and his nephew?" Asked Ramirez.

"Nothing. Alejandro Sánchez and Ruben Pech are still in the wind. We have descriptions but no photos." Toledo replied.

"They might come out of hiding if Fernandez is arrested." Ramirez suggested.

Martinez locked eyes with Cervera, "Will your boss back you, if you and Toledo want to bring down Fernandez?"

Marco's gaze flicked to his partner who tipped his head slightly to the right, signalling his agreement. Cervera casually lifted his cup of coffee to his lips, letting his eyes make a slow circuit of the tiny café, searching for anyone who was a little too interested in their conversation. He leaned forward, set his cup down and lowered his voice.

"In September, Toledo and I were pulled out of an interrogation with Edgar Valdez. He was our prime suspect for the murder of a taxi driver on Isla Mujeres. Both men were low-level dealers for Fernandez on the island." He said.

Toledo added, "Just as things were about to break, our captain sent Marco a text. He wanted to see us ASAP. He said we were now assigned to a more *important* case."

Martinez could tell there was more to the story, so he waited for the detectives to continue.

"Less than twenty-four hours later Valdez slipped in the showers and broke his neck." Toledo's voice held a note of sarcasm.

"We were sure he was about to roll. Give us intel on Fernandez." Cervera said.

"I know he was ready to talk," Toledo grumbled.

"Just bad timing," Martinez said. His eyes said, otherwise. It was a jailhouse pay-off, someone had done a favour for Fernandez.

"*Conveniently* bad timing." Retorted Toledo.

"I'll run this past my boss," Martinez said, "He can put pressure on your captain." Even though he was a captain in the Federal Police, and therefore higher up on the food chain than a captain in the State Police, taking down a drug lord took more juice than he had. They needed some serious backup on this one. Normally the local Navy commander took charge as soon as a drug kingpin was arrested. In Mexico, the Navy brass were believed to be incorruptible, and so far that had proven to be the case.

Martinez eased out a long breath. As much as he respected this group of cops he didn't know them well enough to trust them completely. His beautiful wife Luisa and their five young children were on the island for the wedding festivities. It was time to send his family away to the safe house, a location so secret that not even his best friend Carlos knew it existed.

Life was about to get interesting.

He closed the iPad, "Okay, are we done for now? I am desperate to get a few more hours sleep." He easily lied as he started to stand up. What he planned to do was get his family to safety, as soon as possible.

"Por favor, stay a few more minutes." Cervera swept his hand towards Antonio's chair, indicating the younger man should sit down. "Don't make that call yet. I have an idea."

Antonio slowly sat, holding the other man's gaze. "Okay, what's your idea?" He said watching as Cervera did another visual check with Toledo, verifying his partner was on-board with whatever he was about to say. *Interesting.*

Cervera started with, "This is our backyard. We're local kids. We hate what has happened to our paradise by the sea."

The three others motioned agreement, sadness etched in their features.

Intrigued, Martinez watched as the older cop struggled with what he was about to say.

"I know a couple of guys. Ex-military snipers. They're willing to help."

Chapter 36

February 23rd Late evening Cancun

Towing a small travel bag Jessica stepped off the elevator at the fourth floor, and into an eerily quiet lobby. Three nurses were softly chatting at an enormous work station. One nurse motioned to her own neck indicating she wanted to see the visitor's badge and lanyard that should be hanging around Jessica's neck.

She pulled the plastic rectangle out of her pocket and slipped the cord over her head. To gain entrance to the upper floors she had been required to leave a piece of photo identification with the security desk, and sign the register in exchange for the laminated visitor's pass.

Her eyes swept the length of the hallway, there seemed to only be eight rooms on the entire floor. *It was so quiet it was spooky.*

Any hospital she had ever been in was ridiculously noisy and busy. Visitors and staff talked loudly between each other, or to the patients. There were typically four people per ward unless the patient paid for a private room, even then the doors were left open during the day to accommodate the caregivers coming and going at annoying intervals. This floor was quieter than a five-star Fairmont Hotel.

She pointed at a sign, the room number the security officer had supplied and said, "Mi Tia, my aunt."

The nurse nodded, "Si, claro."

Jessica quietly pushed open the surprisingly thick door to her aunt's room. Despite the weight of the door, it easily swung inward and she stepped inside. The area was as large as a business-class hotel room with a sizable bathroom on one side and a closet on the other side. She quietly deposited the travel bag containing fresh clothes and toiletries for her parents beside the cupboard. She had to walk a few more steps before she could actually see her family; all three of them were asleep.

Heavily sedated Pattie was motionless except for the slight rise and fall of her chest. Despite her numerous freckles she was as pale as the sheet covering her. Jessica resisted the overwhelming desire to fiercely hug her aunt, instead she let her eyes roam over the assortment of blinking monitors, intravenous tubes, drainage lines, waste collection bags and bandages. Sadness enveloped her. *How could this happen to such a good person?*

She studied her parents. Her mom was stretched out on the sofa with a pillow under her head and a cozy blanket pulled up to her neck. Her dad took up every inch of a large recliner, and snored loudly. They looked worn out, shattered.

Jessica shivered and rubbed her arms, then checked the air conditioning control; twenty-two Celsius. Too damn cold for her, but her family didn't seem to notice the chill. She'd bring a sweater next time or she would freeze to death while visiting.

"Hi honey," Her mom said quietly, letting Jessica know she was awake.

"Hi Mom, I'm sorry I woke you," Jessica whispered as she knelt beside her mom and kissed her cheek. "How are you doing?"

"I'm okay. How about you?"

"I'm fine," She fibbed as easily her mother had, "How's Auntie Pattie?"

Pulling back the blanket Anne slowly swung her feet to the floor, and stood up. "Let's talk outside, or go downstairs to the café for a cup of coffee."

Jessica noticed her mom was still wearing the pyjamas given to her by the nurse. She said, "I brought you clean clothes and toiletries. They are in the small suitcase inside the closet."

"Thank you, I'll shower and change after we get a coffee." Anne said. "Besides, I think I look quite fetching in these," She joked, sweeping an arm to indicate her rumpled pyjamas.

Jessica's lips twisted in wry amusement at her mother's attempt to hide her anxiety. "Won't Dad be worried if he wakes up and you're not here?" She spoke as softly as possible.

Her mom carefully checked the information displayed on Pattie's monitors before she answered. "He'll be fine. We've been taking turns popping out for food or to stretch our legs." Anne hunted for her purse, pulled out a few hundred pesos and started towards the door. "The inactivity makes me stiff and sore. I need to move around a bit."

"Bring me a large coffee and something sweet when you come back." Gord mumbled. He shifted his butt in the chair, and wriggled his toes.

Jessica stepped over to her dad, and kissed his forehead. "Hi Pops. Love you." His face was grey with stress and exhaustion. She fervently wished she had never asked them to come to Isla.

"Love you too, baby." He cracked one eye open and smiled faintly.

"We'll be back soon, sweetie," Anne said as she affectionately smooched her husband."

"Take your time, I'm not going anywhere." He closed his eyes, "I *am* getting one of these for our living room." He stated, with a lopsided grin.

Anne rolled her eyes. Jessica smirked. A Lazy-Boy lounger had been on her dad's birthday wish-list for years, but her mom had firmly resisted his frequent hints. She thought the recliners were ugly and old-fashioned. Jessica was certain her dad would win the argument this time.

~

Once they had their coffees and a snack, Jessica and Anne sat at a small two-person table. "Mom, tell me honestly, how is Auntie Pattie?" Her mom wouldn't sugar-coat the prognosis, she would be straightforward and candid.

"Stable, but she'll be in the hospital for at least ten days to two weeks. Then we'll fly her back home to Canada." Anne said. "The bullet nicked one lung, destroyed muscles, and cracked her clavicle." She said, pointing to what was commonly called the collarbone.

"Oh, Mom." Jessica moaned, her eyes brimming with tears.

"She'll have three to six months of recovery and rehab." Anne sipped her coffee.

Jessica wiped the tears from her eyes. "I'm so very sorry that I coerced everyone into visiting me."

"Honey, my twenty-five years of working with medical tragedies has taught me a valuable lesson. You may think you have control over your life, but you don't." Anne reached over and affectionately squeezed Jessica's hand. "Sometimes the good people die, and the evil people survive. Life is random."

Reaching for a handful of paper napkins Jessica noisily blew her nose. The napkins were thin and quickly disintegrated into a sodden mess. She grabbed a second handful, emptying the container and honked loudly.

Anne said, "I'm very thankful that Pattie survived, and no one else was injured. It could have been much worse."

Jessica didn't answer, instead she stood up and deposited the handful of gunky napkins in a nearby garbage can. This was not the time to tell her mom about the second attempt on her life, and Sparky's possible concussion.

"Now, fill me in. What's happening? Will Matt and Jake be coming back tonight?"

"They were both still sleeping when I left the island." Jessica checked the time on her phone, "The last boat to the island leaves Cancun around midnight so they won't have time to get over here, visit and return, so they probably won't come until tomorrow morning. I left them a message telling them I was bringing you and Dad some clean clothes and toiletries."

"Again, thank you so much, for that."

"It's the least that I can do. Why don't you and Dad go back to the island? I'll stay with Auntie Pattie tonight."

"No, thank you, sweetie. We're fine. Neither one of us would sleep anyway." Anne said, "Besides, you have Sparky to think about."

Jessica gulped. *Did she know?*

"He needs to be walked, fed and reassured that you are okay."

"That's all taken care of," Jessica casually answered, masking her relief.

Chapter 37

February 24th Early morning, Cancun

It had all gone to shit! Feet spread comfortably apart, his forearms folded loosely over his chest Alfonso Fuentes stood on a secluded crescent of white sand and gazed at the multi-toned Caribbean Sea. This was his private place to watch the sunrise as it painted the sky with streaks of gold, orange, red and purple. It was his favourite location to think, to plan, and to contemplate life, or to ponder the mess his life had become.

It had started to fall apart just over two weeks ago when a shipment of young Cuban females, destined for the sex-trade, were dumped on Isla Mujeres. They were in the hands of the authorities, spilling their guts on how and why they had ended up on the island.

The young women would eventually be deported back to Cuba to angry, or in some cases disappointed parents who thought their girls had been hired as nannies or housekeepers in the United States. Any off-spring that could earn money was expected to send the bulk of their wages home to help feed and clothe their younger siblings. The parents would not be happy to have the traumatized teenagers back in the family home. *Just one more mouth to feed.*

The captain of the boat Alejandro Sánchez and his nephew Ruben Pech had somehow evaded both the Isla Mujeres policía and the marinas. Sánchez had worked for *Don* Rafael for several years and he fully understood the consequences of failure. The captain had succeeded in warning their large extended families to leave immediately, to disappear. Fuentes knew hiding would be a financial hardship for everyone, but it was better than being dead. For now both men and their families had avoided *Don* Rafael's attempts to locate and eliminate them. Fernandez deemed failure as a personal insult to him, and to his authority. His crews would hunt for Sánchez and Pech until Rafael's hunger for retribution had been placated.

In the meantime *Don* Rafael's lucrative human trafficking business was in a shambles, but he was still a free and obscenely rich man. He had many state politicians, city officials and police officers indebted to him in one way or another. He was virtually untouchable.

Fuentes knew the *jefe* would cultivate new

contacts in Cuba, locate another captain willing to smuggle people to Mexico, and find a secure location for off-loading the cargo.

But more importantly, he was now in personal danger having failed, twice, to kill Jessica Sanderson. The first time, he had shot the wrong woman. That blunder puzzled him. Had he actually missed and hit the aunt by mistake? Or had the aunt unwittingly moved into the path of the bullet? Or had he deliberately not killed the stunningly, beautiful Jessica because he was in lust with her?

His second attempt to execute her had been ruined by her ferocious short-legged mutt, helped by her two brothers who had relentlessly but unsuccessfully chased his motorcycle.

The numerous puncture wounds in his leg from the dog's fangs were hot and puffy with infection. The lump on his head hurt like a son-of-a-bitch. He had stopped at a pharmacy in a scruffy part of Cancun and purchased medical supplies to stem the bleeding. It was the best he could without returning to his home. He needed antibiotics and maybe a tetanus shot, but didn't want to use the doctor they would normally use for questionable injuries. Fuentes had on several occasions asked the doctor to sedate a person on the pretext of giving him an antibiotic injection. A drowsy man was easier to lead to his death.

However, when the *Don* was enraged by failure there was no loyalty among his underlings, it was every man for himself.

Fuentes tensed. He heard car tires crunching over small sea shells, then a car door slammed, and a second one. *I guess my secret location isn't such a big secret.* He mused.

He slowly lowered his arms and turned around, watching the two twenty-something males strut towards him. They were Victor and Ciro the Cuban criminals who had arrived with the September shipment of girls. They were the two men *Don* Rafael had forced to work for him. He said it was the premium price owed to him because his captain had helped them escape the Cuban policía.

Fuentes had distrusted them from the beginning and now here they were, sent by his boss *Don* Rafael. At least Fernandez had enough respect for his talents to send two enforcers to bring in his formerly-trusted lieutenant.

The wolf-pups strode with confidence, spacing themselves a distance apart. Killing one would be easy, but killing two before he died would be tricky.

Fuentes smoothly drew his gun from his waistband, smiling lazily as he held their startled gazes.

Te amo Matías, he whispered thinking of his younger brother as he swung the muzzle towards Victor.

And *both* men silently dropped in a mist of red!

Hijo de la chingada! Crouching Fuentes rapidly spun in a circle but he couldn't spot any other shooters. He dashed for his white Jeep Sahara and jerked open the driver's door. *Por favor Dios.* He turned the ignition key, fully expecting a car bomb to atomize him.

As he spun the SUV in a tight circle, a white piece of paper on the passenger's seat caught his eye. Concentrating on getting away from whatever, or whoever had killed his executioners he ignored the note.

Twelve minutes later he stuffed the Jeep in his secure storage unit. The rolling door pulled down and locked he slumped against the bumper, mentally running through the sequence of events; then he remembered the piece of paper. He reached inside and picked it up.

This is your one chance. We helped you. Kill Fernandez and we will leave you alone — for now. Confirm with a photo to this number.

Fuentes stared at the computer-generated

note printed on plain white paper, his mind buzzing with possibilities.

Another cartel? Gang members? Relatives of someone Fernandez had ordered killed? Cops?

No, not cops. Military. Army snipers. Or ex-Army snipers working for another cartel. But why leave him alive?

It had to be a cartel boss wanting to take over the easy way without a costly war that would terrify the tourists.

Breathing steadily, he mentally mapped out his options. Flight or fight? He had the element of surprise, for a brief time. Fernandez would be confident that he was either captured, or dead. He'd be expecting a confirming text, soon.

It would be useful to have one of their cell phones to text an OK to Fernandez, but he couldn't risk returning to the scene. The cops or the clean-up crew might be there. It was too dangerous to go back.

His pulse thumped reliving the experience; the snuffle of death touching his face like a dog sniffing a new toy.

He would never be safe, as long as Fernandez was alive.

Chapter 38

February 24th Early morning, Cancun

Fuentes eased his Yamaha Road Star into a thicket of plumeria and oleander bushes. He ignored the stiff branches digging into the shiny black paint of his expensive motorcycle. If things went to hell, he had a couple of options to escape but the bike had to be outside the security fence, not trapped behind it.

Conscious of the perimeter security cameras he pulled a baseball cap low over his forehead and tilted his chin down. He sucked in a sharp breath as the cap pressed on his head wound. The cameras were usually checked only when an alarm was activated, but just in case he altered his stride to mimic the rolling pace of an older man suffering from hip-joint pain. He had spent much of his adult life stalking humans, and he quickly realized people unconsciously walked or moved in a habitual manner. Spotting a target was easier when he was familiar with their body movements and posture.

He hoped he resembled the sixty-seven-year old gardener Fido who liked to work early in the morning, the coolest time of the day.

Approaching the service entrance of the complex he punched in his six-digit code. The lock clicked, he pushed it open. *Bueno.* Fernandez was overly confident, and hadn't changed the code. Never again would he refer to that piece of dog-shit as the *Don Rafael.*

He stepped inside, letting the gate quietly shut on the automatic closer. Adrenaline spiking his pulse Fuentes maintained his shambling pace towards the back entrance. The barracks, the common sleeping area, was quiet. The young pups were still in bed, sleeping off a night of booze, drugs and women.

Rafael Fernandez was single by choice, leaving his live-in housekeeper Esmeralda to manage the daily household chores. Fuentes had eaten numerous meals in the cozy kitchen, chatting with her as she prepared his food. He knew she was from Guatemala and as a young child had been sold to Fernandez. In the beginning Rafael has used her for his pleasure but as she matured Esmeralda quickly grasped the concept that she was disposable. She had determinedly created a different and relatively stable life. She became a fantastic cook, soaking up information from cooking shows, books and the few women she met while shopping for food. She accepted the change in her position as stoically as she had accepted being sold to a man older than her father.

Fuentes had watched as Esmeralda had politely endured the rudeness and impertinence of the jefe's young playthings, each one behaving as if she was the-lady-of-the-house until that one was replaced by the next one.

He hoped she wasn't in the kitchen. He liked her, and it would be a shame to kill her, but he couldn't risk her warning Fernandez. Placing his hand on the door handle, he pushed the level down and unlatched the door. He stepped inside and listened. The refrigerator compressor hummed in the stillness.

Resuming his normal gait, Fuentes edged as quietly as a ghost through the hallways, headed towards Rafael's in-home office. A sliver of light escaped from under the door. He pressed an ear to the wood, his target was inside. Without hesitation Fuentes opened the door wide and pointed the gun.

Fuentes fired three shots at Rafael's chest, centre mass in police jargon. He rapidly scanned the room his gun firmly gripped with both hands before stepping inside. Fuentes put a finger to the man's throat, and fired a fourth insurance shot into his head.

"Perdón, I forgot to say buenos días." He said.

He didn't need a long and heartfelt chat with his former employer explaining how disappointed he was that Rafael didn't trust him. That shit only happened in the movies.

Fuentes snapped the photo that his mysterious benefactors had demanded, and hit send. There would be no point in trying to trace the number. It would be a disposable, destroyed as soon as the photo was received. He was on edge. The situation might work out in his favour or it could just as easily swing against him.

First, he had to consolidate his position as the new *jefe*, and then figure out who had saved his miserable ass this morning.

~

Cervera ignored the ping of an incoming message. He and Toledo were in the captain's office updating him on the two recent murders. "We don't have much to go on Capitán." He lied, "We think it was drug related, someone settling a score."

Their captain shrugged, "more dirt-bags, killing dirt-bags. Don't waste a lot of time on it then." He said, waving a hand towards the door, dismissing the men.

"Gracias Capitán." They said, then departed closing the door behind.

Toledo popped his eyebrows up in a question.

Cervera checked the message, turned the screen for Toledo to see the photo.

Toledo twitched a cold smile.

Cervera thumbed a text to two other phone numbers with a single word: Done. He then flipped the mobile over and removed the battery. "I need a good cup of coffee." He said, "You want one?"

"Sure, black, two sugars."

"Back in ten." Cervera said, walking towards the main entrance. Two blocks from the police station he studied the other pedestrians then casually dropped the phone on the ground. He squashed it under his foot, and stuffed the shattered device into an overloaded garbage bin.

As he entered their favourite coffee shop the barista glanced up and smiled. "The usual Marco?"

"Si, dos por favor. Toledo wants black with two sugars." He placed enough money for the beverages plus a small propina, a tip, on the countertop.

Leaning a hip against the counter while he waited for his order, Cervera mulled over what they had done. They had saved one nasty scum-bag to be the executioner of his really nasty, psychopathic scum-bag boss. In time they would arrest Fuentes, but for the moment a shift in power to a marginally less immoral person was preferable to a total vacuum in the cartel leadership.

"Here you go, Marco."

"Gracias Amelia, hasta mañana." He said taking the two delicious smelling coffees. At times he envied people like Amelia who seemed to be oblivious to the murky undercurrents of life.

~

Antonio Martinez heard the soft buzz of an incoming text message. He carefully pulled his arm away from Luisa's warm body, and rolled over. Keeping up with five kids was an exhausting job and Luisa deserved to sleep a little longer.

Laying on his side in the king-sized bed he first checked his regular cell, nothing.

As a cop, he frequently carried more than one cellular; the official one plus a cheap, throw-away. A nervous informant could sometimes be persuaded to call with important information if Antonio vowed the device would be destroyed after their conversation.

Then he picked up the second device and read the text. *Done.*

It was time for a new one. He eased his feet onto the floor, and quietly moved to the bathroom. He removed the battery and the SIM card, then set the device on the counter top while he relieved himself. He tossed the SIM into the toilet and flushed. He would dispose of the body of the phone as soon as everyone was awake and up, but for now he was content to return to bed and snuggle with Luisa.

"Anything important?" She murmured as he repositioned himself against her back.

"Just tidying up a few loose ends." He stuck his nose in her hair and whispered, "It's too early to get up, carina, go back to sleep."

Chapter 39

February 24th Isla & Cancun

Jessica sat beside her Auntie Pattie's bed, lightly holding her hand while she slept. She had finally convinced her mom and dad to return to their hotel room for the night, to sleep on a proper bed, and enjoy a decent meal with a glass of wine, or whiskey or whatever they wanted. Jessica promised to stay with Pattie until they returned. She had all she needed; a couch to sleep on, a bathroom and a café a quick elevator ride away. A nurse brought her fresh linens and at her request two blankets. The air-conditioning was set too low for her tropically-acclimated blood.

Pattie drifted in and out of sleep; exhausted from the aftereffects of the gunshot and the race to save her life. Jessica knew she was also on heavy-duty intravenous pain medication; her mother scrutinized every dose of every drug that was administered. She smiled to herself, her mother might be a pain in the butt to the doctors and nurses, but she was an excellent patient-advocate for her sister.

She felt her aunt stir, shifting a little to ease the constant pressure of the mattress against her skin. Bedsores, the breakdown of the skin tissues, were a common problem with immobile patients even in high-tech hospitals like this one.

The door eased open and her brothers snuck into the room, like two guilty teenagers arriving home well past their curfew. She felt a little flip of love flutter her heart. She missed living close by her family, and she regretted that she couldn't properly share her island paradise with them. Carnaval would start in a few days, but she hadn't reminded anyone of the entertaining event. It just wasn't important anymore. Even the prearranged diving-snorkeling trip with Diego and Pedro on the *Bruja del Mar* had been cancelled. Life was on hold as everyone struggled to comprehend why this had happened.

Why Pattie? Why anyone? Period.

"Hey Jess," Jake whispered bending over to hug her shoulders. "How're you doing?"

"Okay." *Okay but not great.*

"We come bearing gifts for you. Mom sent us on a mission to find you a bottle of wine, a corkscrew and … a proper wine glass." Matt said, pulling the objects out of a pink and white striped

278

bag.

"Now I'm better than okay, I'm good."

~

"This isn't exactly how I planned to celebrate your thirtieth birthday, and our honeymoon." Carlos held up a chilled bottle, "A little more?" He asked.

Yasmin held her glass out for a refill, "We have many years to enjoy our love. Gracias a Dios," she said, sketching the cross over her chest. After the attempted murder at their wedding they had cancelled their honeymoon reservations in Bali, and had booked one night at the Zoëtry Villa Rolandi in an ocean-front suite. The honeymoon could wait. Jessica and her family were more important than a luxury vacation.

"Gracias a Dios," Carlos repeated, more out of habit than conviction.

"Jessica's auntie is improving. She's off the critical list. She's still in serious condition but expected to make a good recovery, in time."

"Si, Jessica said her family is staying until Pattie is released then they are flying back to Canada together." Carlos said, "When they do leave, I am going to upgrade everyone to the bigger seats. Pattie will need a wheelchair and the men are all so damn long-legged; it's abnormal."

He added, with a light chuckle.

"That is very kind of you Carlos," Yasmin smiled at her new husband, a word that she quite liked the sound of, "What a terrible experience for their first trip to Mexico."

Carlos absently nodded in agreement; his attention was focused on Yasmin unconsciously fingering the blue jade pendant, her wedding gift. "I wonder if I didn't tempt the gods a little, with that." He said pointing at the necklace.

"What?" She glanced at the carving she held in her hand, then back at him. "Why would you think that?"

He huffed out a breath, and reluctantly told her about the historical significance of blue jade to the Mayans. He recounted the story that Dante Lopez had told him, how only royalty had been allowed to wear the precious objects, and any commoner found to be flaunting the law was sacrificed.

Carlos ended his story with a slight grimace on his face, uncertain if she would immediately take the necklace off and refuse to ever wear it again, or accept the legend as part of their shared Mayan history.

She stared down at the pendant, then tipped her head up and smiled. "It's beautiful, and I love it. I'm not superstitious" ... she paused, then added, "but I wonder if the priest could bless it for me, just in case."

"I'm sure he would." He said, then lifted his glass of champagne and said, "Feliz cumpleaños carina, Happy Birthday sweetheart." He held her gaze, "To a new and happy life."

"To a happy and healthy life," She gently touched the rim of her glass to his. Across the Bahia Mujeres the Cancun hotels and apartment-complexes were backlit by daubs of gold, orange, red and purple as the sun sank rapidly out of sight. Tropical sunsets happened quickly, and in a few short minutes the spectacular performance would end.

"I feel a little guilty that we're celebrating." His voice was quiet.

"Me too, my love, me too." Her eyes brimming with tears, Yasmin turned to meet his troubled gaze. "But there isn't a lot we can do, except keep everyone in our prayers." She dabbed her eyes with a napkin as she glanced back at the dying sunset. One minute the fiery orb appeared to float in a multi-hued sky, and in the next minute it gathered up the tints and hues like an artist putting away their palette for the day and slid below the curve of the earth.

"Beautiful." She said, wiping her eyelashes.

"Yes, you are." Carlos agreed, moving his head to kiss her. "You are exquisitely beautiful."

"I meant the sunset," Yasmin mumbled under the touch of his lips.

"Was there a sunset?" He glanced innocently over his shoulder to look at the dark ocean.

Chapter 40

March 10th Isla & Cancun

"Good boy, Sparky," Jessica said, smiling as he paddled a short distance. He liked to wade but didn't like to swim. He preferred to feel something solid under his feet.

Sparky, her hero, was stiff and sore for a few days after the kick to his head but he had fully recovered from the ordeal. When she brought him home his sad-eyed stares demanded more attention ... and bits of steak. He'd saved her life. She happily gave him the extra snuggles, and the pieces of filet mignon.

Calf deep in the warm water she stared out at the ocean: reflecting. Her family had flown home to Canada a few days ago leaving behind a large void in her life. She still had her close relationships with what she thought of as her island-family, but she missed the love and laughter of her blood-relatives. As her aunt had steadily improved everyone, except Pattie, had finally taken the snorkeling-diving outing offered by Diego and

Pedro. Behind the smiles and laughter hovered thoughts of Pattie's nearly-fatal injuries, and her long complicated road to recovery.

Pattie's career as a nurse was quite likely finished. She would need full mobility and strength, to continue working. Fortunately she was well-insured and could survive financially but Jessica knew it would be exasperating to her aunt to have limitations in her life. She would fight it, just as anyone in her strong, resourceful family would struggle to regain their independence after a life-altering mishap.

She loudly cursed a long string of profanities in both languages at the stupidity of fate. Sparky looked up sharply and splashed his way back to the shore. He ran towards her, tail tucked and ears down.

Remorseful for scaring her dog Jessica crouched to hug him, "I'm sorry, Sparky. You didn't do anything wrong. I am angry, but not at you."

Somehow she had come to the attention of a vile drug lord and the two attempts on her life had hurt her loved ones; Auntie Pattie and Sparky. Since the incident there had been a noticeable increase in the number of police patrolling the island.

Even the Policía Federal, known as the *Federales* in Spanglish slang, had set up a local office. They conspicuously roamed the island in their intimidating black truck bristling with weapons while three heavily armed constables — head and faces covered by hot balaclavas — sweltered in the hot pickup box. Jessica knew the added security wasn't only because of the attempts to kill her, she wasn't important in the scheme of life. The additional law enforcement was in response to rumours of a Cancun cartel shakeup.

Antonio Martinez had filled her in on a bit of background but she could see in his eyes, he was editing the information that he shared. He was a cop; *un Capitán de la Policía Federal.* He couldn't and wouldn't ever reveal the whole truth. All she knew was an evil man had wanted her dead. According to Antonio, that *pendejo* was dead and another marginally-less evil *pendejo* had taken over as kingpin.

Just fabulous, freaking fabulous. She could only hope the new baddy wasn't even aware that she existed.

~

Fuentes gently smoothed his hand over the satiny surface of the impressive desk, absorbing the feeling of power emanating from the wood.

This was his. He was now *Don Alfonso.*
Señor Fuentes. El Jefe.

Life in the cartel business was normally a
brief and dangerous career. He never imagined
that someday at the age of thirty-three he would
be *the man* sitting behind the desk, not standing
subserviently in front of it.

With a handful of seemingly-trustworthy
supporters, his takeover of the cartel had been
swift, bloody, and effective. Rafael didn't have any
officially recognized offspring or close relatives to
contest the change in leadership so the resistance
quickly fizzled out.

It was common knowledge that two
executioners had been sent by *Don Rafael* to bring
him in, or kill him; but he had miraculously
survived and turned the tables, executing
Fernandez.

The survivors vowed loyalty to Fuentes but
at the same time surreptitiously questioned how he
had pulled off a hat-trick, three deaths and not a
scratch on him.

Let them wonder. He'd take that secret to
his grave.

Ventura Rodriquez Sosa was now his
lieutenant. Aside from his younger brother Matías,
Ventura was the only person Fuentes considered as

a friend, or perhaps more correctly an associate that he currently trusted. Ventura was a smart and ambitious man, one who would need to be carefully watched.

Soon after he had fortified his position as the new boss, Esmeralda the Guatemalan cook, had timidly tapped on his office door.

"Adelante, come in." He'd commanded.

With her gaze pinned to the floor, she asked if she would be allowed to continue her job as housekeeper and cook.

When he agreed, she nervously made eye-contact with him. "Muchas gracias *Don* Alfonso. I am your loyal servant." She'd whispered, placing her right hand over her heart then quickly lowered her eyes.

That was a plus. Esmeralda was a fabulous cook and as a lowly female domestic she was invisible. Even when Fernandez was the *jefe* his crew bitched and complained, oblivious to the woman puttering in the background as she served food and drinks or cleared the empty dishes. But the minute Fernandez stepped into their communal eating-area the men stopped talking or rapidly changed the subject. Yes, she would be a valuable asset.

Fuentes' thoughts turned to another woman. He fiddled with his phone, locating the photograph he had furtively snapped a few weeks ago.

Jessica Sanderson truly was a beauty. The deep blue colour of her dress complimented her wavy blonde hair and stunningly beautiful blue eyes. She had been smiling at her mother, now cropped out of the image. Her open-hearted grin creased her cheeks and lit up her eyes. She was one of those rare women who had no awareness of herself as a female. She didn't have a clue how she affected the men around her. He was fascinated by her beauty, her joy of life, and her sharp wit.

Never in his lifetime would he be able to make a woman like her love a man like him; yet he hungered for her.

El Finito

About the author

Born in a British Columbia Canada gold mining community that is now essentially a ghost town, Lynda has had a very diverse working career. Her employment background has included a bank clerk, antique store owner, ambulance attendant, volunteer firefighter, supervisor of the SkyTrain transit control centre, partner in a bed & breakfast, partner in a micro-brewery, and a hotel manager. The adventure and the experience were always far more important than the paycheque.

Writing has always been in the background of her life, starting with travel articles for a local newspaper, an unpublished novel written before her fortieth birthday, and articles for an American safety magazine.

When she and her husband, Lawrie Lock, retired to Isla Mujeres, Mexico in 2008, they started a weekly blog, Notes from Paradise – Isla Mujeres, to keep friends and family up to date on their newest adventure.

Needing something more to keep her active mind occupied, Lynda and island friend, Diego Medina, self-published a bi-lingual book for children, The Adventures of Thomas the Cat / Las Aventuras de Tómas el Gato. The book won Silver at the 2016 International Latino Book Awards for best bi-lingual picture book for children.

Be the first to know when Lynda's next book is available! Follow her on any of her social media links to get an alert whenever she has a new release, pre-order, or discount!

Wordpress Isla Mujeres Mystery
Facebook Lynda L Lock
Twitter Isla Mysteries
Instagram Isla Mysteries
Amazon Lynda L Lock
Bookbub Lynda L Lock
Goodreads Lynda L Lock
Buy all 3 with one click on Amazon

The legal stuff

The characters and events in this book are purely fictional except the following:

Pattie Packard had the winning ticket at the *Kill Me Off*, Ron Brown Scholarship Fundraiser. As I wrote the story, I realized I couldn't kill a good person and leave her elderly Red Setter Riley an orphan. She survives.

Captain Tony Garcia and his fabulous photos of island life are very real.

The Doctora is vaguely similar to an amazing doctor and dear friend who helped us during Lawrie's illness.

Dante Lopez and the Mr. Opal jewellery store exist.

Yasmin Medina is fictitious, but she is tall with curly hair similar to my friend Yazmin Aguirre.

Jessica Sanderson is product of my imagination. But like me, she was born in BC Canada and she likes critters.

Carlos Mendoza shares a few characteristics with Lawrie; a good sense of humour, the love of dancing, plus the appreciation of Rolex watches and expensive cars.

The *Loco Lobo Restaurant* is completely fictitious, it is not based on any particular location or restaurant.

Temptation Isla
Published by Lynda L. Lock
Copyright 2019
Print Copy: ISBN 978-1-7753788-1-5
Electronic Book: ISBN 978-1-7753788-0-8

Hola amigos y amigas

Pardon my lack of Spanish. I keep trying to learn, but every night while I am sleeping the words leak out of my brain and onto the pillow.

In a perfect world I would have written this story in Spanish or in this case Isla-Spanish which is a colourful mix of local expressions and a bit of Mayan tossed in for added flavour.

However, most of my readers are English speaking. So, for the purpose of this story the local folks are fluent in both Spanish and English, especially the cuss words.

I chose to *italicise* only a few of the less familiar Spanish expressions. For my American fans you will probably notice I spell some words differently. The British-Canadian spelling that I grew up with is what I use.

Like every self-published writer, I rely heavily on recommendations and reviews to sell my books. If you enjoyed reading any of my *Isla Mujeres Mystery* novels please leave a review on Amazon, Goodreads, Bookbub, Facebook or Twitter. Tell your friends, tell your family, or anyone who will listen. Word-of-mouth is enormously helpful.

If you come across an annoying blunder please email me at: lock.lynda@gmail.com and I will make it disappear.

You can also find Sparky and me on social media:
Isla Mujeres Mystery - Notes from Paradise
Facebook @ Lynda L Lock
Twitter @ Isla Mysteries
Instagram @ Isla Mysteries

Temptation Isla

Amazon @ Lynda L Lock
Bookbub @ Lynda L Lock
Goodreads @ Lynda L Lock

Like this book? Please try the others!

Acknowledgements

Writing is a solitary obsession with hours spent creating, considering, and correcting the words on the computer screen.

However, I have had assistance from some amazing people:

- Captain Tony Garcia for the beautiful cover photos for three novels plus the photo of Sparky and me. He is also a valuable source of information about island life.
- You may have guessed by now Tony Garcia and Betsy Snider are good friends. They are owned by several yellow cats, and two dogs. Kitty-Kitty a pale-orange love-bug, is their favourite. Betsy recently mentioned their older dog Deo was the ring-bearer at their wedding. My original plan was for Sparky to carry the ring, but I changed the story. After hearing about Deo, I reinstated Sparky as the man in charge!
- Carmen Amato, mystery writer and creator of the Emilia Cruz Detective Series re-designed the covers for both *Treasure Isla* and *Trouble Isla*.
- Our good friends Diego Medina and Jeff McGahee patiently tweaked the cover for *Tormenta Isla* until I was happy with the results. Diego Medina created the cover for Temptation Isla from one of my photos.
- Patricio Yam Dzul and Aida Yolanda Pérez Martín, plus Freddy Medina and Eva Velázquez are cherished friends who are always willing to share their life stories.
- Apache (Isauro Martinez Jr.) another one of my go-to-friends when I am searching for specific information about the island.
- Dante Lopez for the significance of blue jade to the Maya people
- Doctora Greta Shorey and the Red Cross ambulance attendants who provided irreplaceable

assistance during Lawrie's illness. Thank you for patiently answering my 'well what about this scenario?' questions.

- The incident with Pattie being stuck in a bathroom stall happened to both Val Jukosky and me at the same location —but at different times.
- Val Jukosky, Rick Stearns, Liwlig Larsen, and Damien Lemée are trying to keep the Isla Mujeres Artist Fair alive but it's a tough battle.
- Dianne Stocks and Willow adopted our second rescue dog, Max, in March in 2018. He's a very pampered and happy pooch.
- I used bits and pieces of several Isla Mujeres weddings that Lawrie and I have attended. Thank you, Carly Lancaster and Simon Davison, Deborah Crinigan and Willy Chacon, Mariana Sanchez and Chris Shannon, Marla Bainbridge and Javier Martinez, plus Leanne Miller and Robert Frye for including us in your celebrations.
- Manuscript and proofreaders include, Rob Goth, Julie Andrews Goth, Sue Lo, Betsy Snider, Denise Hawthorne Thorson, Déanne Gray, and Janice Carlisle Rodgers. I truly appreciate your helpful suggestions and corrections, any and all remaining errors are my responsibility. A special thanks to Sue Lo who also did the final proofing.

There are four other groups of people I would like to thank for their continuing encouragement and support:

- Faithful readers of Isla Mujeres Mystery - Notes from Paradise
- Supporters of my children's book, The Adventures of Thomas the Cat;
- Fans of the Isla Mujeres Mystery series;
- And our island friends, ex-pats and born-here-locals who patiently answered my questions about this and that and everything.

Thank you, thank you, and thank you all!

Celebrate your love

Photographers:

Tony Garcia: https://www.facebook.com/CapitanTonys
Captain Tony Garcia is a fabulous photographer for any event including weddings, engagements, and family reunions. His charming photographs of daily life on Isla are a treasure for future generations. Tony is also a well-informed tour boat captain, taking visitors to Isla Contoy, swimming with the whale sharks during the summer season, and snorkeling.

Julie Fraga: http://serendipity-design.com/#home
On an island as small as Isla Mujeres you would think that Julie and I would bump into one another more frequently. Busy with our creative endeavors we occasionally have time for a squishy hug and a quick update on our lives. Julie crafts fabulous photographic memories for any occasion, and designs excellent webpages.

And two more recommended photographers:
Cecilia Dumas:
https://www.facebook.com/CeciliaDumas.Photography/

Susan Pacek:
https://www.facebook.com/susan.pacek

Event Planners:

Sun Horse Weddings: http://sunhorseweddings.com/
I have seen Tiffany Lanier and her remarkable team in action a number of times. They have their own in-house catering staff available for events at beach clubs or private homes. Here's a quote from her webpage.
"Getting married in paradise should be fun. The Sunhorse Wedding Team has planned over 400 custom weddings on this idyllic Caribbean island. We specialize in private events and rent venues on Isla Mujeres exclusively for you and your guests, so you can get

married on a private beach surrounded only by your friends and family."

Palm Atelier:
https://www.facebook.com/ThePalmAtelierEvents/
Quote from owner Jana Mattox: "We take care of every detail and will make your event one to remember. We specialize in planning the design, the style, and flow of your event from concept to clean up! We don't sleep, so that you will. Our boutique service can create your dream destination wedding, a corporate retreat or celebration, a fundraising festival, vow renewals or even a special engagement or honeymoon week."

Weddings Isla Mujeres:
http://www.weddingsislamujeres.com/
Quote from isla-mujeres.net: "The sister team of María and Kin have found the perfect fusion of old-world Mexican charm and the rich tradition of Isla Mujeres to create what has become one of the region's most inviting beach wedding locations. Your seaside wedding is customized, so no two are ever alike. "Have fun. Make it yours. Cherish it while it's happening!"

Hair and Makeup:

Ursula Lopez Salon:
https://www.facebook.com/ursulalopezsalonservices/
Amaranta Ancona Cervera:
https://www.facebook.com/Estética-Amaranta-Beauty-Salon

Flowers:
Florería Hortencia: Beautiful arrangements and bouquets. They have been located in Centro on Avenida Francisco I. Madero #7, for many years.

Cakes and Goodies:
Sugeidy Avilés & Sugeidys Café: Yummy!
https://www.facebook.com/sugeidyscafe
https://www.facebook.com/pastrycocoacupcakes/

Nubia Magaña Galué
https://www.facebook.com/nubiamaganagalue/

Cake Island:
https://www.facebook.com/cakeislandmex/

Venues:
Depending on the size of your group the event planners recommend the following locations:
Javi's Cantina & Dinnertainment, Rosa Sirena's Restaurant & Rooftop Palapa Bar, El Patio Caribbean Grill, and Rooster Café. Plus Zama Yacht & Beach Club, Zama Chachacha Garden, Capitán Dulché Beach Club, and Playa Lancheros.

Venues with accommodations for small groups:
Casa Sirena Hotel in Centro is my favourite boutique hotel. It is available for groups of fourteen or less. If you book all six guest rooms you will receive their best price. There are a number of multi-bedroomed rental houses on the island available for groups. A little research on the internet will bring up several rental agencies available to help you.

Venues with accommodations for larger groups:
Hotel Paradise Suites-Isla Mujeres, Playa Arena, Ixchel Beach Hotel, Privilege Aluxes-Adults Oriented, Nautibeach Vacation Rentals, Izla Hotel.

Legal or a celebration of love?
Unless you complete all the legal forms usually with the help of your event-coordinator your *Acta de Matrimonio* is not legal outside of Mexico, it is a spiritual celebration of your love. You will have to be legally married in your own country, perhaps at a simple civil ceremony just to get 'er done!

For readers who are a little Spanish-challenged

Bruja del Mar – Literally witch of the sea, Sea Witch
Carina – urban slang for a funny, gorgeous, and amazing girlfriend
Casita – small house
Casa – house
Chucka-chucka – humorous Mayan euphemism for sex
Cómo está? – How are you?
Con permiso – to move around or past a person
Don or Doña – respectful title used with the person's first name
Hermano – brother, or any male who is like a brother
Hermana – sister, or any female who is like a sister
Hijo de la chingada – crude curse, son of a bitch
Hola – hi or hello
Hombre – man
La Trigueña – The young woman Mundaca loved
Loco Lobo – Crazy Wolf, also El Loco Lobo but one of our Mexican friends said Loco Lobo sounded better
Maldito – darn, damn
Mama - mom
Mami – mommy
Mande? – The person didn't hear you.
Más o menos – more or less
Mi amor – my love
Mierda – swear word, shit
Mordidita – bribe, literally a little bite
Motos – motor scooters, motor bikes
Niña(s) – girl or girls

Niño(s) – boy or boys, can also mean children
Papa - dad
Papi – daddy
Pendejo – swear word
Que pasa – what's happening
Que pasó – what happened
Pícaro – horndog, randy male
Rapido – rapid, fast
Testamentos – wills
Tía – auntie, or an older female who is like an aunt
Tío – uncle, or an older male who is like an uncle
Topes – speed bumps

Sparky and his writer

Made in the USA
Monee, IL
28 January 2020